TEARS
of a
PATRIOT

TEARS
of a
PATRIOT

An American Warrior in Vietnam

John E. Siipola

PAGE
SOLUTIONS
PROWRITERS NETWORK

"He jests at scars that never felt a wound..."
<u>Romeo and Juliet</u>, Act 2 Scene 2, William Shakespeare

The characters in this novel are fictional. This novel is based on stories that I heard from my brothers, friends, and classmates. Thirty years ago, I couldn't recount these stories without personal distress. Now, it is a different lifetime, but the hurt still lingers.

2,594,000 men and women served within the borders of Vietnam and 58,148 were KIA (killed in action) and another 75,000 were disabled. Two-thirds of those who served in Vietnam were volunteers. Most say that they are glad to have served their country and would serve again.

Some of our veterans were flown home after their tour of duty and arrived stateside some 36 hours from combat. They were very happy to have survived and were going home. They had done their job. Done their duty for God, honor, and country. Proud to have served their country, but were met with disdain, taunts, and worse when they arrived in the good old USA. Their peers who were deferred for college or grad school or those who went to Canada, or elsewhere to avoid service, derided them and many later have gone on to be successful teachers, professors, and politicians.

Only about 2% of our population now has had military experience. They haven't seen the elephant as the combat veterans say. Combat is intense with terrifying explosions so close that you lose your wind and water. A dead body in the heat will be crawling with maggots within hours and within a day it will be black and bloated. The sights and smells in the aftermath of combat will never be forgotten by those who have lived through it and neither will the hurt of our veterans that have been disrespected by the very people enjoying the freedoms that they fought to preserve.

To all who were there, thank you for your service.

John E. Siipola

TABLE OF CONTENTS

CHAPTER 1

Austin, Texas

September 1961

He came in with his head low and his eyes fixed on his target. My legs couldn't move fast enough to avoid the collision with his lean, two hundred pounds of bone and gristle. It was the first football game of my junior year at the University of Texas. As a safety on defense, I received the kick off and met Tommy. We were both running on adrenalin with some 60,000 classmates, alumni, and fans watching at Texas Memorial Stadium. The tackle could be heard in the second deck of the stadium in Austin. Tommy Herndon was a hard-hitting linebacker for Southern Methodist University. Me, Jack Stryker, I was just a back-country half-breed on a life changing scholarship to play ball, get a degree, and get out of a depressing hometown where my future would be pretty dim. Tommy and I met several more times that afternoon. He was the kind of linebacker that just seemed to be in on most plays. He loved contact and hit like a pile driver. We played against Southern Methodist again in November and I knew that we would meet head on several more times before the season ended.

Tommy's parents had a ranch, started by his great-grandfather, outside of the city of Austin and I had seen him occasionally around town. Too bad, he went up to Dallas to SMU for college instead of joining the Longhorns here in Austin. I'd much rather have him on my side. Over the Christmas break, I went to the San Jacinto Café, about a block from the state capitol building, for dinner. Tommy, had come home from college for the holiday, was there with his date. Tommy recognized me as I walked in by myself and beckoned for me to come over to his table.

"Hey, Indian, how come you're not home for Christmas?", Tommy said.

I just murmured, "Couldn't make it."

It was probably transparent that I could neither afford to go home for the holidays nor did I really want to go back to Pinedale, Wyoming in mid-winter. He introduced me to his date, Babs Foster, a stunning, tall blonde, and asked me to join them at their table. I felt awkward, but Tommy prevailed and we shared football stories over dinner. Tommy and I agreed to meet the next day at the weight room to train together. I had no real reason or money to go home to Wyoming for Christmas. I was glad to have some companionship. Since I was hanging around campus over the holiday break, Tommy and I met a couple of times and then he invited me out to his parents for Christmas dinner. While I did my best to avoid him every time we played, we had formed a bond of friendship off the playing field. It was the beginning of a long and close friendship between us.

Tommy was the well-loved, outspoken Texan most of us picture as the son of successful, third generation Texas ranch owners. High, wide and handsome, Tommy was an all-around good guy. He was a year older and a class ahead of me.

Tommy's parents lived on a ranch in the hill country about 15 miles south of Austin. He drove a neat '56 Corvette that was white with a red leather interior. He had the mannerisms that suggested some family affluence, but I wasn't prepared for the ranch when I arrived for dinner with his family. As I pulled off Route 35 in my old Mercury Monterey with cowboy plates from Wyoming, the black Angus cattle were grazing in a field with three oil rigs slowly rocking back and forth. They pumped up the underground wealth of Texas. The ranch house looked like a fairy tale mansion to me. Then, Tommy introduced me to one of the nicest, most loving families that I had ever met - his parents and kid sister, Carole.

Dinner was more like a feast. Wild turkey that Tommy had shot last week and tenderloin from a Black Angus steer that had been butchered and aged for 18 days. After politely answering their questions about my native American heritage and family back in the Wind River Range of Wyoming, Tommy's dad, Chester Thomas Herndon, call me Chet, suggested that Tommy take me for ride in the family's single engine Eurcoupe, a low winged two-seater airplane that could fly low and slow, to see the ranch. They had a grass strip runway out behind the horse barn.

I walked around the airplane following Tommy as he did his pre-flight check. It was obvious to me that he knew what he was doing and he patiently explained the pre-flight and its importance to me. Tommy directed me to the right hand seat. The little Eurcoupe just barely contained the two of us. As Tommy let the engine warm up, he checked the controls and radio. Satisfied, he pushed the throttle forward and taxied out to the end of their private grass air strip.

The little airplane bolted forward when he pushed the throttle full forward and we easily climbed up in the blue Texas sky.

After two hours of air time I had seen most of the Circle H ranch that covered almost 12 sections or about seventy-six hundred acres of rolling Texas hill country.

My dad guided big game hunters in the fall and trout fisherman in the spring, so I grew up hunting and fishing in the back country of the Wind River Range. The number of little Texas white-tailed deer on the ranch impressed me. Tommy said the quail hunting was pretty good, too, and I had an open invitation to come up during the fall hunting season.

Tommy brought us back to the grass landing strip behind the house just as the winter sun was setting in the southwest. As I said my thank you's and goodbye's, Tommy's parents invited me back whenever I wanted home cooking. Just call first to make sure they were home. Driving back to the Crow's Nest, the Navy ROTC house where I lived just off-campus, I continued to feel the warmth of the Herndon family. I was also very glad that Tommy would graduate in the spring and wouldn't be on the SMU team when we played them next football season.

I visited the Herndon ranch over spring break for three days rather than going to Splash Days in Galveston where many of my classmates went. I really had no attraction to a week of bacchanalian trolling for female companionship along the beach. Tommy's little sister, the strawberry blonde Carole, was a big attraction closer to Austin. I made myself a solemn promise to be a proper gentlemen and not to embarrass any of the Herndon family. Tommy was looking forward to playing pro ball and was drafted by the Oakland Raiders. Joining him for his daily workout schedule, helped get me into great physical shape for spring training when I returned to school.

CHAPTER 2

The Oakland Raiders

September 1962

When Tommy joined the Raiders for the 1962 season. Oakland had finished the '61 season with 2 wins and 12 losses in the American Football League. Roman Gabriel, a quarterback from North Carolina, was their number one draft pick. Tommy just made the roster. His aggressive play was one of the few highlights for the team in an otherwise dismal year. The Raiders finished in last place winning only one game. They beat the Boston Patriots 20-0 in their last game of the year on December 16, 1962, with only 8,000 fans in attendance. Head coach Red Conkright was replaced by Al Davis for the 1963 season.

At the end of the school year, I became a Midshipman 1st Class in the Navy ROTC unit. I was in the regular NROTC (Navy Reserve Officers Training) program that paid some of my college expenses not covered by football and provided a much needed midshipman's pay of $75 a month in spending money. Each summer, midshipman from the 52 colleges that had contract and regular NROTC programs went on 6 weeks of ACDUTRA (Active Duty Training). Those cadets that elected Marine Corps option or volunteered to be commissioned as second lieutenants in the Corps upon graduation went to beautiful Camp Quantico to run the perimeter and learn how to become members of the green gun club. The rest of us who were destined to become Ensign in the USNR (the regular Navy, USN, was reserved for academy grads who automatically received higher numbers for future promotion ranking). We Midshipman got more pleasant ocean voyages for our initiation to the ranks.

That summer between my junior and senior years at UT, I went on my 1st class midshipman's cruise. With my ROTC classmates, we flew on a MATs flight (Military Air Transport) out of Bergstrom Air Base in Austin to San Diego. I joined the U.S.S. Rogers DDR-876, a destroyer converted to a radar picket ship. The Rogers was named after the five Rogers brothers who had served with distinction in WW II. My assigned task was to qualify as Junior Officer of the Deck.

Most of us looked forward to the summer cruise as one of the highlights of the NROTC program. This was my 3rd summer cruise. Adjusting to shipboard life as a very junior officer was easy. I knew my way around destroyers. I was well briefed in the routines of Fire Control, Combat Information Control (CIC), Anti-Submarine Warfare (ASW), and the responsibilities as JOD (Junior Officer of the Deck). The 6 weeks flew by as we cruised from San Diego to San Jose, Guatemala; then to Rodman Naval Base in the Canal Zone; through the Panama Canal to Cartagena, Columbia. We were invited to play basketball at the Columbian Military Academy and had use of their gym. We put together a reasonable pickup basketball team. Seven tall enlisted crewmen and me. Then we sailed on to Belize, British Honduras where we were invited to the British Army Base.

We spent two days anchored off Belize and then on through the Cuba Deep where we encountered a violent storm that we plowed through for another two days. We took some water in the forward stack 102 feet above the waterline. It was quite an initiation to the power of the sea. After the storm passed, it was a quiet ocean as we passed by Key West on the way to Mayport, Florida. The Captain rotated me through each department with a syllabus to chart my progress and hone efficiency in every area to prepare me for active duty next year. The XO (Executive Officer), Lieutenant Gale, checked my qualifying task list daily. This time next year, God willing, I would be an Ensign and be permanently assigned to similar duties.

I returned to Austin at the end of July. Suntanned and fit, I was back at UT the last week in July at the Crow's Nest, the Navy ROTC house or coop where I bunked during the school year. Everyone else had gone home. I had no desire to go home to Wyoming, I loved my parents, but Pinedale was just depressing and I was on a very limited budget. The guys that I had played ball with in high school that were still there were working at hard manual labor jobs or drunk or both. Jerry Redcloud, the catcher on our baseball team, who had caught my fastballs since Little League, got shot last year in a drug trade. Mom and Dad understood why I had little motivation to visit home.

Tommy and I had stayed in contact. He had become my Spirit Brother and as close as any big brother could have been.

With football practice just a week away, a good workout at the gym and then a swim out at Barton Creek where the local girls hung out seemed a great way to spend the day. I called Tommy who was home from training camp and he said he'd be there by early afternoon.

Tommy had added twenty pounds of muscle through weight training and nutrition since I saw him last. He had been drafted by the Oakland Raiders and had some playing time last year. He had just two days at home before going back to the Raiders pre-season training. Tommy picked me up in his Corvette and we went out to Barton Creek. Tommy mentioned that his parents had given him orders to invite me out to the ranch for dinner. After ogling the local bathing beauties, Tommy drove me back to the Crow's Nest to change.

It was a beautiful summer day in the Texas hill country. Riding out to the ranch in Tommy's Corvette with the top down was as good as it gets. His kid sister waved from the swimming pool as we pulled up to the sprawling ranch house. Carole was just a kid, a junior in high school, but cute as a button with strawberry blonde hair and freckles. Cute now, but with the promise of becoming drop-dead gorgeous. Her clear, blue eyes had that sparkle of life and I was hopelessly infatuated. Limited good judgment and the start of football practice tomorrow got me safely off the ranch before I made a fool of myself. At their invitation, I became an occasional weekend visitor during my senior year. They became my surrogate parents and I admired Carole from distance. She did invite me to watch her cheerlead for the Stephan F. Austin high school team and took great pleasure in showing me off as the UT football player that was friends with her big brother, the pro football player. I maintained control, barely, and really enjoyed watching her grow up that year.

My senior year at UT blew by really fast. Tommy was getting some playing time in the NFL. His parents became huge Raider fans and spent weekends flying out to see Tommy play for the Raiders. We stayed in touch and sometimes got out together when he was home. Tommy had now bulked up another 15 pounds of muscle. He said the Raiders had a great weight trainer that put them all on a really high protein diet that added bulk. I guessed that some steroids were included that could account for the rapid muscle growth and weight gain. Tommy was now huge at 250 pounds on his 6 foot 3-inch frame.

We beat Oregon 25-13 in our first football game in Austin on September 22nd. We traveled to Lubbock to play our second game against Texas Tech on the September 29th. It was a blow out. We won 35-0, but I blew out my knee. I had torn the medial collateral ligament in my left knee early in the game.

I watched from the sideline on January 1st as we lost to 7th ranked LSU 13-0 in the Cotton Bowl. The 26 story Mirabeau B. Lamar Library, named after the former President of the Republic of Texas, was not bathed in victorious Texas burnt orange to signify a win, but the parties went all night anyway.

Getting around on crutches was boring, but it eliminated some of the distractions and gave me the opportunity to study more and improve my GPA. By March, I was playing some easy basketball and lifting at the gym. Several of my team mates had been drafted by the NFL. I had a commitment to serve my country and became Ensign Stryker in the United States Navy upon graduation in May. I had every intention on becoming a career officer.

1963 was the Raiders fourth season in the AFL. Al Davis changed the team's uniforms from the original gold and black to silver and black. Tommy started the first game of the year at the Houston Oilers. He made his bones and they won 24-13 astonishing the odds makers. Tommy was fast becoming a defensive star as the Raiders won 10 games and finished in second place. Quarterback Cotton Davidson went to the Pro Bowl. Al Davis was named coach of the year and Tommy was on his way to becoming future franchise player

CHAPTER 3

Fitting In—
Norfolk, Virginia

January 1964

After almost seven months as Ensign Stryker, the Navy bureaucracy is something that I have yet to fathom. I spend my time reading administrative reports at FRAM II (Fleet Rehabilitation and Modernization) in Norfolk, Virginia and supervising the administrative work of Big Chief Thurlow. Thurlow, Clinton F., CWO-4 (Chief Warrant Officer 4) has 26 years of varied experience in the U.S. Navy. He knows everything about our duties and responsibilities. I am convinced that he knows everything about everything.

I'm bored. I have the utmost respect for the Chief. He has counseled me on how lucky I am to be stateside in a safe and soft billet as Southeast Asia is heating up and presenting some international challenges. But most of my days start with a workout to maintain some physical fitness, a shower at BOQ (Bachelor Officer

Quarters), then a slow morning at the office, followed by lunch, and a slow afternoon at the office. An evening at the Officers Club just compounds my boredom. The occasional ball or event at the O Club, with required attendance for junior officers, only meant that I need to uncomfortably wear the starched white uniform designated Tropical Dress Long with the tight, semi-turtle neck collar or the Navy Blue Dress Uniform in the winter. Of course, the officers' wives could not stand a young, athletic-looking officer staying single and unattached. I have met most of their younger sisters, cousins, and unattached friends. Not all bad, but I haven't met the right one yet. And, I suspect that their interest fades as they learn of my dirt poor, Native American heritage. Yes, I sense that there is some East Coast class conscientiousness. I still have memories, most probably fantasies, of Tommy's kid sister, Carole Herndon.

Tommy and I still write to each other on a regular basis. He had met Gwen Gunderson in January, in Las Vegas. Gwen, at six feet tall in flats, was almost Tommy's height. Gwen was a striking blonde who had an established acting career in Hollywood. Tommy had found the girl of his dreams. He had just signed a five year, multi-million dollar contract with the Raiders and had the world by the tail.

Gwen liked to party and Tommy went along. He was completely and hopelessly in love with the lovely Gwen. Tommy wrote that he and Gwen would be traveling to the east coast and would like to stop in Virginia and meet me for dinner on their way to New York. He and Gwen were enjoying life and partying hard in the off-season. We met at the Hunt Room located at the Cavalier Hotel in Virginia Beach. Gwen was even more beautiful and vivacious in person. Tommy and I were interrupted often by Gwen. It seemed to me that she needed to keep herself in the center of our discussion. I passed it off as her need as an actress to be in the center stage. It was great to see Tommy again and for us to get caught up. I wished them all the best as the left to catch a charter flight to New York.

I can expect my duty assignment in Norfolk to last another five months. At 23 years old, I want to feel like I'm carrying my own weight and need some action. I have trained for sea duty in the black shoe navy. I'm fit, ready, and feel like I'm wasting my time and the government's dollar.

Today may be a turning point in my naval career. The Big Chief has known of my sense of uselessness and hands me a request for transfer to a special school that had just been set up.

Chief Thurlow said, "Think long and hard about signing it. Captain Reed, the four striper that runs FRAM II, will most likely approve your request to transfer to Naval Special Warfare Preparatory School."

This was a nine-week program to determine if candidates could pass extreme physical conditioning to potentially qualify for a new unit. This new small unit operations group will morph the legendary Navy frogmen into sea, air, and land operations. It means nine to twelve months of very arduous training that includes underwater demolitions, jumping out of perfectly good aircraft, and something they call "Hell Week". The Chief then cautions me that it would be highly likely that future assignments would be "in harm's way".

Three years earlier, President John F. Kennedy, aware of the situation in Southeast Asia, recognized the need for unconventional warfare and special operations as a measure against guerrilla warfare. In a speech to Congress, Kennedy spoke of his deep respect for the United States Army Special Forces.

In 1961, Arleigh Burke, Chief of Naval Operations, had recommended the establishment of guerrilla and counter-guerrilla units. These units would be able to operate from sea, air or land. This was the beginning of the Navy SEALs. All SEALs initially came from the Navy's Underwater Demolition Teams, who had already gained extensive experience in commando warfare.

The first two teams were formed in January 1962 and stationed on both US coasts: Team One at Naval Amphibious Base Coronado, in San Diego, California and Team Two at Naval Amphibious Base Little Creek, in Virginia Beach, Virginia. Men of the newly formed SEAL Teams were trained in such unconventional areas as high-altitude parachuting, demolitions, and foreign languages as well as advanced hand-to-hand combat. The SEALs attended Underwater Demolition Team (UDT) replacement training and they spent some time undergoing intense physical training. Upon making it to a SEAL team, they would undergo a SEAL Basic Indoctrination (SBI) training class at Camp Kerry in the Cuyamaca Mountains east of San Diego. After SBI training class, they would enter a platoon and then conduct platoon training.

According to founding SEAL team member Roy Boehm, the SEAL's first missions were directed against communist Cuba. These consisted of deploying from submarines and carrying out beach reconnaissance in prelude to a proposed US amphibious invasion of the island. On at least one occasion Boehm and another SEAL smuggled a CIA agent ashore to take pictures of Soviet nuclear missiles being unloaded on the dock.

The Pacific Command recognized Vietnam as a potential hot spot for unconventional forces. At the beginning of 1962, the UDTs started hydrographic surveys and along with other branches of the U.S. Military, the Military Assistance Command Vietnam (MACV) was formed. In March 1962, SEALs were deployed to South Vietnam as advisors for the purpose of training Army of the Republic of

Vietnam (ARVN) commandos in the same methods they were trained themselves.

The Central Intelligence Agency began using SEALs in covert operations in early 1963. The SEALs were involved in the CIA sponsored Phoenix Program where it targeted key North Vietnamese Army personnel and Vietcong sympathizers for capture and assassination.

The SEALs were initially deployed in and around Da Nang, training the South Vietnamese in combat diving, demolitions, and guerrilla/anti-guerrilla tactics. As the war continued, the SEALs found themselves positioned in the Rung Sat Special Zone where they were to disrupt the enemy supply and troop movements and in support of riverine operations. Most of their missions were on the inland waterways.

There was very little information available on this new unit, but I needed a change. I completed my application for training.

As the Chief had indicated, Capt. Reed approved my request for transfer.

Orders came through in March for me to undergo PRE-BUD/S training in California. I knew that the next nine months would test my physical capability and mental resolve. I said good bye to the Big Chief and thanked him profusely for all his help and guidance.

He said, "Stay safe, son and God be with you."

In pre-season workouts for the 1964 season, Tommy had lost a step. He was still a big, hard hitting linebacker and faster than many competitors, but he had Gwen as an outside interest. He spent just a little less time working out and more time partying. September 13th opening day, Tommy was clipped from behind and blew out his left ACL as the Raiders lost to the Patriots 17-14.

Surgery to repair his ACL and intensive rehab forced him to sit out the season. Gwen continued to party hardy. The end of their relationship was inevitable. By the end of February, Tommy was back in shape and at a decision point in his life. Coming from a politically astute and patriotic Texas family that had a long history of military service, he was well aware of world events. Several of his friends from home and college were serving in the military, including me. We had stayed in contact. I had followed his football career in the papers and we exchanged letters or telephone calls pretty much monthly.

On Wednesday, March 3, 1965, Tommy made his decision at the Marine Corps recruiting office in Austin. His Dad had served with distinction in the Marines during the Korean War. Tommy joined the Marine Corps.

He wrote to me from Basic Training. The Marines were sending him to Officer Candidate School following Basic Training. He expected to be commissioned Second Lieutenant USMC in July.

CHAPTER 4

Joining the Team

May 1965

SEAL training was more demanding than double sessions under Coach Royal at UT in the August heat. It is not designed to get you into shape. You have to be in exceptional physical shape to survive. By design, the training program will stress you beyond your limits to prepare you for the extreme physical and mental challenges of small unit operations in combat situations.

PRE-BUD/S, a 9-week Apprenticeship Training Division School (A-School), is immediately followed by assignment to BUD/S (Basic Underwater Demolition / SEAL) training. BUD/S was a seven-month training challenge that develops your mental and physical stamina and leadership skills. Each training phase includes timed physical condition tests, with the time requirements becoming more demanding each week.

"Hell Week" is the defining event. It is held early on. First Phase – before the Navy makes an expensive investment in SEAL operational training. Hell Week consists of 5 1/2 days of cold, wet, brutally difficult operational training on fewer than five hours of sleep. Hell Week tests physical endurance, mental toughness, pain and cold tolerance, teamwork, attitude, and your ability to perform work under high physical and mental stress, and sleep deprivation. It tests determination and desire. Only 25% of SEAL candidates make it through Hell Week, the toughest training in the U.S. Military. Candidates realize that they can do more than they ever thought possible. They know that they will never, ever quit, or let a teammate down. I had somehow survived "Hell Week". It began on Sunday and ended on Friday.

After completing initial SEAL training, there is advanced training, which includes foreign language training, SEAL tactical communications training, Sniper, Military Free-fall Parachuting, Jump Master, Explosives, and much more. Training, physical conditioning and drills are part of the SEAL lifestyle.

Finally, graduation came and I had made it through the program. Five of us were commissioned officers, 4 ensigns and a lieutenant junior grade. I would be designated as a Platoon-Officer-in-Charge.

Lieutenant Junior Grade Jack NMN (No Middle Name) Stryker was now officially a member of SEAL Team One and proudly wore the Special Warfare insignia of a golden eagle clutching an anchor, trident, and flint lock pistol. It is one of the few warfare specialty pins that is the same for officers and enlisted. It symbolizes that Navy SEALs are brothers in arms. They train together and fight together.

The anchor symbolizes the Navy, the parent service. The trident, the scepter of Neptune, or Poseidon, king of the oceans, symbolizes a SEAL's connection to the sea. The pistol represents the SEAL's capabilities on land - whether direct action or special reconnaissance. If you look closely, it is cocked and ready to fire and should serve as a constant reminder that SEALs must be ready at all times. The eagle, the nation's emblem of freedom, symbolizes the SEAL's ability to swiftly insert from the air. Normally, the eagle is placed on military decorations with its head held high. On the SEAL insignia, the eagle's head is lowered to remind each of us that humility is the true measure of a warrior's strength.

I was anxious to meet my platoon of trained SEALs.

I was officially assigned to SEAL Team One, based in Coronado. SEAL Team One had responsibility for the Pacific Region. My unit, the 4th Platoon, was part of the Naval Special Warfare Group and was already scheduled for deployment to Southeast Asia. The SEALs represented less than 1% of the combined services personnel. It was an elite fighting group trained to be agile mobile, and hostile.

My platoon was comprised of two 5-man squads. I was Platoon-Officer-in-Charge. Alpha Squad comprised squad leader, Guadanoli, Joseph, CPO (Chief Petty Officer) USN, Geary, Joseph L., PO-3 (Petty Officer 3rd Class) USN, Rivera, Jose J., PO-1 (Petty Officer 1st Class) USN, White, Richard F., SSgt. (Staff Sergeant) USMC. Bravo Squad included Collins, Mitchell R., PO-1 (Petty Officer 1st Class) USN, Jones, Jeremiah J., PO-1 (Petty Officer 1st Class) USN, Castanaro, George E., PO-1 (Petty Officer 1st Class) USN, Connell, John L., PO-2 (Petty Officer 2nd Class) USN, Keane, Earl K., PO-3 (Petty Officer 3rd Class) USN. Much later a typical SEAL platoon would be comprised of two squads of six men each.

The two most senior team members of my platoon were Guadanoli and Collins. They had already been deployed to Southeast Asia as Advisors in guerilla warfare. The rest of the team except for Jones had just graduated with me from SEAL training. Jones was a class ahead of us and had been on medical leave. He had broken his leg on leave after graduation. While almost all SEALs were in the Navy, a few Marines were team members. The Marine Corps and

Navy were considered sister services both reporting to the Chief of Naval Operations. Our lone Marine, SSgt. Rick White, was a huge Black-American from Alabama. He had been recruited from Camp Pendleton several years earlier to assist in developing the physical training program and just stayed with the SEAL program.

My platoon began Advanced Training as a unit. Sniper training, explosives, and, of course, physical conditioning for two months. I was now Lieutenant Junior Grade Stryker and Platoon-Officer-in-Charge. Guadanoli and White had individually let me know that I was in their very capable hands. I recognized and respected their experience and let them know that I readily accepted all assistance. They were already seasoned warriors.

At the end of July, we completed Advanced Training. It was no surprise that we were ordered to Vietnam. I called a platoon meeting to let the guys know. Guadanoli and Collins volunteered information on what we could expect based on their tour in-country as advisors to the ARVN (Army of the Republic of South Vietnam). After the meeting, I went to the base library to research South Vietnam and, specifically, the Mekong Delta region where I expected that we would be spending most of our time.

The military had designated the delta area as the Rung Sat Special Zone made up of two districts, Quang Xuyen and Can Gio. The Rung Sat Special Zone Headquarters was located in Nha Be in the Gia Dinh Province and was responsible for about 485 square miles with over 3,000 miles of interlocking streams and canals. There was an estimated population of 18,000 Vietnamese fisherman, woodcutters, and farmers. The South Vietnamese Navy and our Mobile Riverine Force or Brown Water Navy patrolled these waterways.

CHAPTER 5

Time to See the Elephant

August 1965

My Platoon joined some 165 Marines aboard a commercial Continental DC-8 Super Six airliner. August is the middle of the wet season in South Vietnam. Daily temperatures average in the mid-90's with high humidity dropping into the 70's at night. It rains virtually every day. We landed at Tan Son Nhut airport in Saigon. I had expected to hear the sound of gunfire, but it was relatively tranquil. As we exited the ramp, the hot air immediately caused a soaking sweat that trickled down my armpits and soaked my fatigues. The heat waves rose off the tarmac and the afternoon clouds promised rain. South Vietnam has two seasons. The dry season runs generally from November to May and the wet season from June to October. This was August and we could expect high humidity and precipitation every day.

The Marine newbies, fresh from Basic Training, that joined us for the flight over to Saigon all milled around the open walled tents for processing. The oppressive heat and humidity carried the smells of airplane fuel, exhaust, and sewage. The terminal had evidence of general neglect. I had expected to see tracers and in-coming as we landed, but it was just hot and smelly. There were no sounds of mortars or combat. Except for the dilapidated buildings, we could have been in Houston, Texas.

Being one of the few officers that disembarked, I was quickly informed that my platoon was assigned to the Mobile Riverine Base at My Tho in the Rung Sat Special Zone. There were six buses in line beyond the tents. We were assigned to the first bus in the line. The driver, a Marine corporal named Whitney, opened the door and a blast of cold air greeted us from the air conditioner turned up to max. The A/C was not standard issue. Whitney had rigged up a unit for his own comfort. Man, that felt good. So far we had no contact with the local population or any menacing events.

The image changed quickly as we pulled out of the air base. We passed through two check points and entered a street busy with every sort of transportation from bicycles to diesel trucks. We had about a 70-kilometer ride southwest on Route 1A that got rough and a bit hairy as soon as we were outside the city. A slow 2 hours later, we arrived at our base camp in My Tho. It was strategically located at the junction of Route 4, a relatively good road that traversed the delta, and not far from the confluence of the My Tho and the Tien Rivers some 80 kilometers upriver from the South China Sea. It was also close to Kien Hoa Province that was known as the home of the communist Viet Cong National Liberation Front (NLF).

The bus pulled into the guarded entrance to the base. The base personnel were housed away from the waterfront where the River

Patrol Unit and their boats and support equipment were located. The foot traffic inside the gate included many Vietnamese mingling with the U.S. Marines. We got off the air conditioned bus and gathered up our sea bags and weapons and were met by a Marine Gunnery Sergeant. GySgt. Rose showed us to our tents called hootches over here. He said that I could get settled in before reporting to his boss. The Marine Force Recon and SEAL platoons both reported temporarily to a Marine, Major Cashin. The Vietnamese were referred to as either gooks or dinks. There were dinks everywhere. My hootch that I shared with Lt. Joe Mazzaroli from Massachusetts, included a gook maid. The Gunny said all hootches had a maid that would cost us 30 piasters a day or about 28 cents. The maid worked cheap and would clean and make the beds. They needed a security card to gain admission to the base. It struck me as a perfect way for the VC to get inside information on our troop strength and supplies, but no one else seemed bothered by it. Being the newbie, I kept that to myself.

Major General Lewis Walt was the recently appointed Marine Corps commander in Vietnam. General Walt was in his early fifties, but still looked like the linebacker he had been at Colorado State. He reported directly to General Westmoreland, Commander U.S. Forces in Vietnam. One of his objectives was to chase the Vietcong and NVA (North Vietnam Army regulars) out of the populated delta areas. It was a tedious and painstaking campaign to rid the hamlets of sympathizers, political cadres, and guerillas.

SEALs were initially deployed around Da Nang to train the South Vietnamese in guerilla and anti-guerilla tactics. Later, SEALs were deployed in the Rung Sat Special Zone to stalk the Vietcong in the Mekong Delta. My team had the mission to reconnoiter, locate, and destroy VC personnel and supply caches in the delta and to interdict the enemy's lines of logistical support. The SEALs objective was to own the Rung Sat Special Zone, the vile swamp in the Mekong Delta. I vowed to myself that the Vietcong or Victor Charlie, Charlie for short, would venture onto my turf at his own risk and I would attempt to make that a very high risk.

Our base in My Tho was at the edge of the Rung Sat Special Zone with the high rice plains to the north and Cambodia about 125 kilometers to the west. My Tho is the capitol city of the Tien Giang Province located about 70 kilometers southwest of Saigon and about 30 kilometers from the East Vietnam Sea. Our base camp was near the confluence of the Tien and My Tho rivers. During French colonial times My Tho prospered and the remnants of that era were still visible. Once three separate kingdoms, Vietnam was drawn together under French colonization late in the 19th century. The north was industrious and populated mainly by the Tonkinese. The south was more laid back and agrarian populated mainly by the Cochinese in the fertile Mekong Delta rice bowl.

There are several islands in the river south and west of My Tho and the Gunny warned us that we could experience in-coming rounds when the VC infiltrated the islands within mortar range of our base camp.

The first night in camp a mortar round exploded at 0100 hours. I jumped up and pulled on pants and boots as several explosions rocked the base. It was over quickly and I was told by the old timers that the gooks owned the night. I decided that I would always sleep dressed with my boots on. Ready for action. I was now in-country and my job was to follow orders and keep my team alive. I also told myself that we needed to learn how to operate in the night.

Orders for my platoon came down from General Walt to the Battalion Commander, Colonel Albert "Bud" Langer, U.S. Army.

Col. Langer was Special Forces and the Phoenix Coordinator with the CIA, and then to Major Cashin. Major Richard Cashin was in charge of the Marine Force Recon units in the area and we reported to him temporarily until LCMDR (Lieutenant Commander) Zanke, the SEAL officer-in-charge, returned from the states. SEAL capabilities were not always appreciated by the regular Army or Marine Corps. SEAL teams were still new and vaguely understood. The Phoenix Program had been in operation since the beginning of 1965 and had been designed and coordinated by the Central Intelligence Agency with the Special Operations Forces.

The Phoenix Program's objective was to neutralize (via infiltration, capture, terrorism, torture, and assassination) the infrastructure of the National Liberation Front of South Vietnam (NLF) and Viet Cong. The two major components of the program were Provincial Reconnaissance Units (PRUs) and Regional Interrogation Centers. PRUs would kill or capture suspected NLF or Viet Cong members, as well as civilians who were thought to have information on NLF activities. Many of these people were then taken to interrogation centers. Many were tortured in an attempt to gain intelligence on VC activities. The Regional Interrogation Centers, run by the CIA, were very effective and used torture because it worked. The information extracted at the centers was then given to military commanders. Torture nearly always worked. The information was extracted and then corroborated from another source before being used as potentially reliable. If the information provided proved erroneous, executing the informant in front of the other prisoners usually stopped the flow of erroneous information.

First Sergeant Harry Wallace let me know at breakfast that I was wanted at Battalion HQ right now. I immediately canned the rest of breakfast and followed Wallace to HQ. As I entered, the Colonel said, "Good morning, lieutenant, is your team ready to pull your own weight here?"

"Ready for your orders, Sir."

"Delta Company's First Platoon engaged a company size group of NVA Regulars last night at coordinates 21908. Take your team to scout the area and cover them as they return to base. They have a prisoner and are tired and low on ammo. I am concerned that the NVA may counter attack and air support is not available right now."

Major Cashin, who had some familiarity with our training, remained silent as the Colonel was asking us to play nursemaid to his proven resources in the field.

Looking for a positive spin, it would acquaint us with the area.

Seeing Guadanoli coming out of the mess tent, I asked him to assemble the platoon and be prepared to disembark within 30 minutes as I reviewed the area map. I had attempted to tactfully explain to Wallace, who I assumed had the Colonel's ear, that we had significant cross-training. From his look, it was obvious that he believed that we were just newbies.

It was a long uneventful walk to 21908. Delta's First Platoon, led by Lt. Downs, was policing the area as we arrived. They had a good night with no wounded, referred to as peanuts, and no KIA's. They killed 2 gooks that he called dinks and captured a wounded NVA officer. My platoon circled the area. The signs of combat and 2 gook bodies were all that we found. Our first up close view of our enemy. They were just over 5 feet tall and very slim. The bullet riddled bodies were not very imposing and beginning to bloat. They were covered with flies in the hot mid-day sun.

We had a long walk back to base as the afternoon rain shower soaked us and made it slippery underfoot. I reported in with my after action report.

The Colonel didn't quite know what to do with a SEAL Platoon and Major Cashin was busy with the Phoenix Program. We spent the next two weeks playing body guard both to the units on patrol and the Navy riverine activities. Heavy rain showers were a daily occurrence.

There was a ten boat River Division based at My Tho. It included a repair facility, spare parts, fuel barrel tank farm, and ammunition stored in shelters. The Navy Riverine units used Patrol Boats, River (PBR's) and Patrol Boats, Fast (PTF) otherwise known as Swift boats to inspect river traffic, transport and extract teams in the Mekong Delta known as the Rung Sat Special Zone. The PBR was a versatile fiberglass hulled boat with a shallow draft of 2 feet and water jet drive to operate in weed choked rivers. The drives could be pivoted to reverse direction, turn the boat in its own length, or come to a stop from full speed in a few boat lengths. They were manufactured in two versions, the first with 31-foot length and 10 foot, 7-inch beam. The Mark II version 32 feet (9.8 m) long and one-foot wider beam had improved drives to reduce fouling and aluminum gunwales to resist wear. They usually had a 4-man crew with either an ensign, LTJG, or a Petty Officer First Class as captain. PBR's were powered by dual Detroit Diesel 6V53N engines with Jacuzzi Brothers jet drives. They could reach 32 mph. Ordnance included twin .50 caliber machine guns forward in a rotating shielded tub, a single rear M60, 7.62 mm light machine guns on each side (starboard and port), and an MK 19 grenade launcher. The crew also carried onboard a full complement of M16 rifles, shotguns, .45 ACP hand guns, and grenades. The hulls were not shielded by armor since they relied on speed and maneuverability.

The larger 51 foot Swift boats had twin 960 HP General Motors diesels and a crew of six (an officer and 5 crew men). Weapons included an 81-mm mortar and three .50 caliber machine guns. They were made by Seward Seacraft in Louisiana and originally used in Cuba.

I loved riding the boats and mingling with their crews. In my first 3 weeks in-country, I had not fired a round in anger. My platoon was eager to get into the action. Both Guadanoli and Collins had experience in-country and cautioned us to be careful and patient.

The powers that be soon learned that these PBR's were ideal for inserting and extracting small teams to create havoc far from our base. My SEAL Platoon started to really earn our keep when we could hitch a ride far up or down river on a PBR interdict the VC supply route, blow up their cache of food, medical supplies, and ordnance and quickly be extracted by river. We learned that night operations and silently slipping in and out leaving corpses and booby traps inflicted significant psychological impact on the enemy.

Major Cashin informed me that he believed that a VC camp was in the palm forest just southeast of My Tho. Some information gained from the Phoenix Program indicated that this camp had supplies of ordnance and medical supplies that were distributed to VC forces and sympathizers in the area. The trail leading from My Tho along the river to the camp was bound to be watched and probably booby trapped, but a PBR could ferry us down the river and insert us quietly where he pointed to the map at a bend in the river. We would insert in the dark and hit the camp in the pre-dawn hours.

We reviewed the logistics and then I laid out our plan to guys. When I asked if there were any questions, Geary replied, "No problem, Lt. It's a moon light cruise and some action before breakfast."

The PBR throttled down and quietly idled into the river bank. It was a clear night in the mid-70's. We disembarked and climbed up the gentle slope of the river bank. We double checked our weapons and moved into the coconut palms that grew along the river. White took the point and we moved out in single file.

We figured the deep rem sleep time was about 0300 hours and that's when we wanted to hit the camp.

We arrived right on schedule. One of the camp dogs caught our scent or picked up a sound and began barking. We were in the brush about 20 meters from the camp spread in a semi-circle on the north and east sides.

Another dog trotted out to join the first and began barking. Shouts in Vietnamese followed. An armed VC stepped out of the hootch nearest the dogs. Guadanoli cut loose with his M60 and we poured fire and launched grenades into the camp. Three or four VC managed to escape into the trees from the southernmost hootch that was the farthest away from us.

It was a short firefight. Thanks to our readiness and the enemies complete surprise we had suffered no casualties.

We maintained defensive positions until the first rays of daylight provided us with some visibility. On my signal, Alpha Squad moved through the camp. The hootch walls were no protection against our incoming fire. All nine inhabitants were dead from multiple gunshot or shrapnel wounds. We searched the bodies for any potential intelligence. There was a significant stockpile of M40 rockets, grenades, and boxes of 7.62x39mm ammo for AK-47s. We counted 15 rifles. I thought I had seen 3 or 4 VC run out the other end, but based on the number of rifles it may have been as many as 6 VC that had escaped.

I called for extraction. We burned the camp and destroyed the ordnance as we awaited the PBR to take us out. I thought about how the escapees would tell their tale. We had come silently in the night.

The psychological impact might be greater than their loss of supplies and personnel.

The VC would begin to fear the "Green Faces", their name for us because of the green camouflage paint that we used to cover the shine of our faces.

After a shower and change of clothes, I reviewed the action with Major Cashin. He agreed that the mission plan provided a blueprint for our next mission. We would follow a similar approach with another identified camp east of My Tho up the Tien River.

Major Cashin closed the meeting by saying, "Lt. get your platoon rested and I 'll schedule the insertion with the River Rats."

The River Rats were the Mobile Riverine Support units or Brown Water Navy that operated the patrol boats. They were no boats available until tomorrow night. I met with Petty Officer Campbell who would be in charge of PBR-33 tomorrow night. His boat was being repaired after being hit by small arms fire earlier. Campbell assured me that his boat would be repaired and he would personally check it out before our scheduled departure. After we inserted, he assured me that he would be nearby on patrol and PBR-33 would be available for our extraction on short notice. We reviewed the planned insertion and extraction to our mutual satisfaction.

With Campbell at the helm, the PBR nosed into the muddy bank of the Tien River. We stepped into the ankle deep mud and slogged in water half way to our knees into the brush. We only had about a kilometer to cover to reach the camp. The maps had indicated dry ground, but the river was running high and we waded about half the distance in a foot of water. Getting close to the camp, we finally reached slightly higher ground. It had been slow going and I wanted to hit the camp before dawn.

I took the point to set a stealthy and quiet approach to the enemy camp. It was slow going and we would arrive later than I had planned. As I reached the camp's clearing, the dark night was just giving way to the gray pre-dawn and the birds and critters began their wake up calls. I motioned for the squad to their positions. Guadanoli with his M60 was closest to the river and the sampans tied there. We expected that when he opened with full automatic fire that Geary and Rivera would have a clear kill zone to the east and Collins and I would have the northern escape route covered.

In combat chaos and the unexpected happen more often than not. Guadanoli's automatic fire into the first hootch resulted in screams. Women and children poured out of the other two hootches yelling with their arms raised. We cautiously approached the group keeping up our guard. We found two dead in the first hootch along with an AK-47 and some explosives and materials to manufacture step on mines for booby traps. I called in for extraction and then ordered the women and children to the far edge of the camp's clearing. We burned the hootches and shot holes in the hulls of the sampans. These were NLF (National Liberation Front) sympathizers.

CHAPTER 6

My Tho

September 1966

The 1st Battalion 5th Marines were operating in the Rung Sat Special Zone southwest of Saigon. A Vietcong sniper or snipers had been consistently harassing Marine patrols about 104 kilometers or 65 miles south of Saigon along the My Tho River. The sniper had accounted for 6 KIA's. Young Marines that would never go home. Marine snipers and the Marine Force Recon units were very good at their job, but had been unable to find the sniper or snipers. There was a shortage of deployed Marine snipers, so we got the job to find and eliminate the VC sniper activity.

We boarded a PBR at oh dark thirty. Our platoon of 10 men plus the 4 crew men made the 31-foot boat sit a bit lower in the water, but the twin diesels got us up on a plane quickly. I estimated that were skimming along at about 25 knots. Our plan was to be inserted upriver of the target area where the sniper had been operating. We carried 70 pound packs, extra ammo and MRE's. Since we expected that we would out for several days, we would schedule our extraction after we eliminated the sniping activity.

We disembarked from the PBR at 0715 hours after an uneventful ride. Checking our gear after climbing up on dry ground, we moved out on a southeast tangent to the river. Guadanoli's squad took the east and I went south, closer to the river with my squad. We would sneak and peek to learn the area and the habits of the local VC. By late afternoon, we had found old sign, foot prints on some trails that we crossed, but nothing recent. Finding a small brush covered area of high ground, we rejoined Guadanoli's squad and decided that we would bivouac for the night. First, we had to find where they lived. I strategized our next day's plan with Guadanoli, my Bravo Squad Leader. We carefully reviewed our maps and noted two areas to reconnoiter tomorrow. Again, each squad would take a separate route. Reconnoiter the assigned target area and then meet up to plan the next step.

Collins had the first watch as the platoon settled in for dinner. No fires, just MRE's and water. Castanaro would have the next turn and then Geary would be on watch until 0400.

It was all quiet until Geary had a scare on early morning sentry duty when three pigs came through the brush and passed about 5 meters away. The wild pigs in Vietnam were tastier than MRE's, but we had to be quiet and could not give away our presence by shooting one for dinner.

After a quick, cold breakfast, we saddled up to move further to the east searching for signs of the sniper or VC activity. Only about 250 meters east we came upon a small village that sat in a little valley with a stream or canal running along the south side. Guadanoli's squad was just off on the far side of the village about 50 meters further east. The ligh0t prevailing wind had kept the sounds and smell away from us. We sat on the edge of a small brush covered hill and watched the villagers begin their agricultural workday. By mid-morning, most of the villagers were out in the fields. I was getting fidgety and I knew that the platoon was getting anxious. I motioned for the platoon to move in and search the hootches for weapons.

Guadanoli's squad would cover us as we searched the hootches. The village kids ran out laughing and chattering to greet us, but as we got closer they stopped and became quiet. We were the dreaded Green Faces.

We fanned out and looked into each hootch. The village was clean. No weapons found. As we started to leave, a young man probably 13 or 14 years old motioned us to follow him down the trail. About 75 meters down the trail, he pointed down. Sure enough, Sgt. White found a "Step-On" mine. Geary and Castanaro found three more. I thanked the young man and handed him two chocolate bars from my pack. That's all I had.

The "Step-On" mines were hand made by the VC by filling an empty .50 caliber shell with gunpowder or other explosive powder and scrap metal. The casing was then sealed in wax and placed in a bamboo cylinder with a nail in the bottom, which is then buried in the ground so only the wax on top is showing. When a person steps on the wax top the casing is pressed into the nail which then blows scrap metal into the soldier's foot and legs. Not usually fatal, but bloody, nasty, and disabling.

We changed our plan of the day and kept the two squads together staying off the trail. Working each side of the trail, we resumed our reconnaissance of the area. The humidity was rising. It was the rainy season. It was hot, muggy and the difficult going made more difficult because we needed to be quiet and stealthy. After a short noon-time break, we worked our way further south. I figured that we were about

12 kilometers northwest of Binh Dai. The Marines had targeted this area as the sniper's operating turf.

The trail forked with one trial heading due south and the other fork going east. Guadanoli would take the south fork and my squad would go east. We reviewed the maps and agreed to meet up around 1800 hours at a small rise about 2 kilometers further southeast between the trails.

Picking our way along in the brush beside the eastern-most fork of the trail, our point man, Castanaro, signaled a stop. We watched two bicycles with baskets full of the colorful local fruit grown here by the villagers. Local fruit included Dragon Fruit, Star Apples, Papaya, and Mangoes. I guessed that they were going to market in Binh Dai. It also was a really good indicator that this trail wasn't booby trapped.

We continued to parallel the trail for another two hours, but there was no more traffic. It was time for us to work our way west to the small patch of higher ground that we had designated as our meeting place and meet up with Bravo Squad.

Finding the small hill in this flat, heavily brush covered terrain was a navigation challenge. I called Guadanoli, "4-Bravo this is 4-Alpha, we are at 216780".

"4-Alpha. We have you in sight."

His squad had made the rendezvous spot a few minutes ahead us. Guadanoli would not let me forget that I walked right into them. So much for my indian skills.

By pure luck, this was an excellent spot to keep watch. We overlooked a trail that according to the map led to a village down by a tributary that ran to the main river. Guadanoli reported that this trail split off from the south fork that he had followed. If the sniper was from that village and headed north looking for an early morning target, then just maybe we would be in the right spot.

I had the mid-watch from 2400 to 0400 hours. I relieved Rivera a few minutes early. It was about 70 degrees and raining. I sat with my poncho draped over my shoulders. My boonie hat kept some of the chilling rain drops off my neck, but I had to keep my ears uncovered to pick up any sounds in the night. I had only been on watch for about an hour when I could detect a faint rustling in the brush. Something was moving off the trail and approaching up the small hill toward us. The rustling in the vegetation would pause for long moments and then move a bit. It was either a pig or a gook and it was getting very close. The movements were too stealthy to be wild pigs rooting for food. There was no appreciable wind, but there was movement in the brush and it was now only 5 meters to my left. The movement was about shoulder high, not a pig or a wild critter. I pumped three quick rounds of 12-gauge buckshot into the movement and then dropped to a prone position in the mud in case of returned fire. No further noise or movement.

Staying in position, I looked over my right shoulder. I could make out the platoon wide awake and watching the perimeter. There was a faint noise of something or someone retreating to the trail south of my position.

The platoon was on high alert. Not much sleep for any of us tonight. I stayed quiet in the dark listening to the rain drops hit the vegetation and trying to discern any other sounds. As the dawn slowly provided some visibility, Castanaro quietly came up to me and we crept out to survey the area.

Where the brush had moved last night, we found a dead black pajama clad young woman of about 20. The buckshot had had mangled her torso. Next to her body was a Russian made Nagent 7.62x54mm scoped sniper rifle. The sniper or at least one sniper had been eliminated. The muddy tracks indicated that her spotter had run off to the south and there was a blood trail. One of my shots had clipped the spotter.

I motioned to the platoon to follow and began tracking the spotter. By mid-morning the sun was out. It was hot, but my Shoshone ancestors would be proud. I was still on the trail. It was getter harder to follow. A broken branch here and there. A drop of blood every once in a while. A print from a sandal further on. It was slow going. I was confident that I could find where the spotter went, but I was also concerned that we could walk into a trap.

At 1115 hours, the tracks intersected a road that went to a village about 200 meters further east. Sneaking and peeking our way through the brush, we got into position around the north and east sides. The road curved at the village and then ran to the south. West of the village was a large cultivated field with limited cover that went all the way to the river. Most of the village inhabitants would be out working in the fields, but the spotter and any remaining snipers would most likely be resting in one of the hootches.

I motioned for Guadanoli's squad to provide backup cover because he had the M60 machine gun.

As my squad cautiously spread out and moved into the village, a little black pajama clad figure carrying an AK came out of a hootch to White's right. The big man was quicker than the gook and a 3 shot burst dropped the gook a step from the hootch. Castanaro tossed a M61 hand grenade into the hootch. A gook popped out of the last hootch on the left, Guadanoli's M60 cut him down.

We searched the rest of the hootches and found three AK-47's, about 100 rounds of ammo, and a dozen grenades. Since we found no other sniper rifles, I concluded that we had killed the lone sniper. This was a VC village and I ordered it burned. The villagers had come in from the fields. The mama sans and kids were unarmed and excitedly chattering at us in Vietnamese. I motioned them to stand quietly with hands behind their heads as Bravo Squad covered them with their weapons. We burned each hootch where we had found weapons. They began wailing and screaming at us.

I wanted to put some distance between us and the burning village before our extraction. We headed north up the trail parallel to the river and I called for a PBR pick up. It would take about two hours for the boat to get here and I picked a spot that we could comfortably reach in that amount of time. Fortunately, the trail stayed parallel to the river and we reached our extraction point with fifteen minutes to spare. Guadanoli volunteered to take the watch while the rest of the platoon took a break.

Fifteen minutes came and went. The boat was running late. We all knew that any VC's in the area would be motivated to find us. Finally, the PBR radioed us just as they came into view. As it nosed into the bank, the platoon hustled onboard. The chief in charge of the boat goosed the engines and just as we turned upriver a 40mm rocket skipped behind the stern. The VC's on the shore opened up with AK's and a few rounds punched into the starboard gunwale. The Gunner's Mate opened up with the forward twin .50 caliber machine guns and we sped away before they could launch another rocket.

Our good luck was holding. We counted coup as my Shoshone ancestors would say and had no casualties. As the end of the wet season approached, we began experiencing violent thunder storms and torrential downpours. We were forced to curtail our activity, sometimes for several days. The water table crept higher and higher. High tide, even this far upriver, could inundate the fields and leave almost impassable muck as it receded. We rode with the Swift boat crews during the bad weather to assist them in boarding suspected

Viet Cong supplies on the river. They were very happy to have us perform as the boarding party relieving them of this dangerous activity.

Alpha Squad was on a routine patrol onboard a PCF Swift boat heading upriver from My Tho toward Ca Be. The boat captain, LTJG (Lieutenant Junior Grade) Dan Weeks, had taken some small arms fire from the east side of the river two days ago and warned us that we could expect more incoming from the shore as we passed that area just south of Cai Be. The captain kept us near the middle of the river and had us at full throttle as we approached that area. Sure enough some small arms fire buzzed by us as we passed. The Swift boat had twin .50-caliber Browning machine guns located on the centerline on top of the pilothouse. The gunner was ready and returned fire. The twin .50's had a range of 7,000 yards were capable of firing some 500 rounds per minute. They were far more effective than the small arms on shore. The captain said that this was a daily exchange and that he had no idea how much damage that the boat had inflicted on the shore battery.

Approaching Cai Be, we sighted a small motorized junk coming downriver hugging the western riverbank. The morning fog provided some cover along the shoreline and this just looked suspicious. The captain immediately decided that we should investigate and maneuvered the 50-foot Swift boat to intercept the junk. Alpha squad checked their weapons and we prepared to board as we came along side.

As we approached to about 100 meters, the VC junk foolishly opened fire at us. The gunner on the twin .50-caliber Browning's immediately responded decimating everyone and everything on the deck of the junk. The boat captain expertly brought us alongside and Alpha squad jumped onboard as the PCF crew fixed lines fore and aft to the junk. We searched the bodies of the four dead VC splattered onto the deck. Multiple .50-caliber wounds made a real mess. After collecting their papers, we found ordnance stashed below. Ammunition, grenades, and rockets that would not reach the Viet Cong villages in the Tien Giang Province.

The captain had two crewman board the junk and set a towline to haul it back to the Mobile Riverine Base at My Tho. We were all on alert approaching the area where we had received incoming fire earlier coming upriver. Our speed was largely reduced towing the junk and I felt like we sitting ducks at a carnival rifle gallery. We chugged by the danger zone with no incoming. Maybe the morning's exchange of gunfire had reduced or eliminated the shore battery's capability. Our luck was holding.

CHAPTER 7

River Duty

October 1965

By October, we were now viewed as old timers and our capabilities had been tested. We were fully recognized by the command as very capable predators. We were becoming legendary to the locals. The VC called us "green faces: and put a bounty on any green face killed. To claim the bounty, a gook had to return with the head.

We were blooded and feared. I also knew that we had been very lucky since none of my team had been killed or seriously wounded. SEAL Commander Roland Zanke had been appointed to command the SEALs in Vietnam and was now in-country. The Navy had established several SEAL support bases in South Vietnam including a major upgrade to our base in My Tho.

Cmdr. Zanke visited My Tho arriving yesterday afternoon. He met with my platoon, the Marine Force Recon platoon and Major Cashin representing Col. Langer. The Commander was very interested in the river pirates that were assumed to be on Thoi Son. a large island south of My Tho on the Mekong River. The VC pirates, as he referred to them, were interrupting trade and fishing. They were also surmised to be a supply chain for the VC that were sending mortar rounds into the Chau Thanh District on a regular nightly basis.

It was clear that a night insertion onto the island was in our future. Thoi Son was about a 45-minute boat ride down river beyond the confluence of the Tien River. The island is about 11 kilometers long and a little over 1 kilometer wide. Guadanoli, Collins, and I researched all maps available, including those captured from the VC, to locate a landing site for our insertion.

The island grew fruit and coconuts. Foliage was thick and a floating group of sampans were anchored on the west side. The river zig zagged and had a relatively secluded potential insertion point on the northwest tip. There were several creeks that ran through the island mostly lined with palm trees and thick undergrowth. After insertion, we would sweep the island to the southern end and then work our way up the western side.

The game plan was to sneak and peek. Create psychological havoc by destroying targets of opportunity. A 51-foot Swift boat or PBF would patrol the river from My Tho to Ap Vinh Hoi to interdict the pirate activity. Another riverine patrol unit would cover from the river mouth up to Vinh Hoi.

After lunch, I briefed the platoon on our mission. We would board a PBR just before dark at 1800 hours for insertion while there was still some visibility for the boat crew.

Our insertion went undetected and we quickly found island travel meant wading creeks and hacking our way through thick undergrowth until coming upon a trail through coconut palms and fruit trees. October weather is characterized by violent thunder storms and estuary flooding in the delta. In the stygian darkness the thunder rolled in followed by a downpour. I knew that the tributary streams that crisscrossed the island would become raging with strong currents that could make them very difficult to cross.

Slogging through the mud and seeking high ground we had stumbled into a plantation that had several out buildings and a substantial main house, perhaps a remnant of the French Colonial era. The road in front of the main house lead west from the plantation most probably toward the anchorage and floating market on the west side of the island.

Our point man, Connell, signaled a halt. Guadanoli signaled for us to move back into the shadows. I was in the rear and could not make out any threats. The squall line had passed and the rain stopped.

The sound of an M60 machine gun broke the evening's silence. At least three AK's chattered in response followed by the explosion of two grenades close together. The building received a steady stream of fire. Then, we quietly moved back in the underbrush.

After we moved back, Guadanoli reported, "Lt there was a mortar squad of four gooks exiting the house. We eliminated them with the first burst of fire. The incoming fire came from three windows in the house. Rivera and Jones were able to toss M61's (grenades) into two of the windows."

"Well done." It was all I could say since I was shielded by the brush from all the action. I wanted to put at least a kilometer between us and the plantation before dawn. A good night's work. One less VC mortar squad and perhaps two more dead or wounded gooks inside the house.

Our luck was holding.

Before dawn, we found a secluded spot. Jones had the first watch and we settled in for some needed rest. Keane would relieve Jones and in four hours we would have a cold meal and then continue carefully moving north along the west side of the island.

By late afternoon, we were approaching the floating market and village on the west side of Thoi Son Island. The sizeable village could have several thousand inhabitants including the boat people in the floating market. Conferring with Bravo Squad leader, Chief Guadanoli, we decided to stay back in the bush and observe the area until the village retired tonight. We would try to determine supply locations or where they had ordnance stashed that we could destroy in the darkness.

As we waited and watched in the twilight, a sampan came to the shore landing. Five gooks began unloading the boat. We could make out some rockets along with many boxes with unknown contents. I guessed that they contained ammunition and grenades. The gooks formed a line to off-load the supplies. Another line assembled to carry the materiel to an open sided hootch with a thatched roof.

That would be our target for later tonight.

Rivera volunteered to sneak in to the supply hootch and set C4 explosives to destroy the cache and we would cover him from the edge of the brush. We would watch the village until the it was quiet in the post-midnight hours. I planned our route to an extraction point that we could reach after dawn and called in the estimated time and coordinates. I wanted a PBR waiting there for us. I expected that we would be heavily pursued after the VC figured out what had caused the explosion.

I was concerned that many factors could go wrong. Both Guadanoli and Collins were optimistic that Rivera could creep in and set the charges without detection because the supplies were stored so close to the river bank and away from the village and the anchored sampans. I wanted to have the platoon extracted before a major retaliation force could be assembled.

At 0345 hours Rivera crept in and set the explosive charges with a time delay of 20 minutes. We covered him from the edge of the brush. No dogs barked and no gooks came out for an early morning piss. Guadanoli set a trip wire trap behind us to slow down any pursuers on the narrow trail leading away from the village that we followed to our extraction point. We were almost to our extraction point when the supply cache exploded.

Before long the first streaks of daylight filtered through the clouds. Our ride back to My Tho had not arrived on schedule. We took a defensive position beside the small foot trail that we had come down. It was always an anxious time before extraction knowing that we were being pursued. We had set trip wire traps back up the trail as an early warning system to let us know if the VC were getting close. We got a call that the PBR had come under fire, but was on its way. We waited. As daylight filtered into the trees around us, the colorful little birds, parakeets and some kind of finches flitted in the trees. The adrenaline seeped out of me and I fought to stay awake and alert. I heard a distant explosion. It was the booby trap that Guadanoli had set outside the village. The VC had figured out what had happened and where we went.

Our good luck held. The PBR arrived and we were skimming our way back to My Tho before the VC force found us. The Green Faces had won again.

Our first night back at My Tho, the mortar attack began on schedule at 0100 hours. After about 4 hours of interrupted sleep, I had our orders to catch a ride northwest about 14 kilometers up river. There was VC activity reported in the area between Route 864, which ran parallel to the Mekong River, and the river shore where

Route 870 split to the north. My platoon was to reconnoiter and potentially destroy any materiel caches that we found. We resupplied our ammo and grabbed some MREs. We were ready.

River Division 53 based in My Tho had, at the time, 4 Alpha boats that were in constant demand. Campbell was the Navy Petty Officer First Class who captained the PBR known as Dragonfly Alpha-3. Captain Campbell got the word for our insertion and was expecting us. The twin engines were fired up and the exhaust gurgling in the brown river water as we boarded for our journey upstream.

Campbell quickly got the boat up on plane and maneuvered the PBR to the center of the river to mitigate the effectiveness of small arms fire from either shoreline. We skimmed along in a light rain. At a speed of 25 knots the rain soaked through everything before we reached our insertion point just east of the Route 870 intersection. Campbell eased the boat in bow first to the shore and we were able to step ashore with our equipment.

We checked our weapons, shouldered our packs, and moved out. We had ventured inland to Route 864 when the rain got very heavy and visibility was limited. We hunkered down under our ponchos waiting for the rain to let up. We needed at least some visibility to effectively reconnoiter.

The rain didn't let up. It was a downpour that went on until just before dawn. The rain finally stopped and the morning fog was thick. We moved out staying south of the road. The map showed an inlet west of the Route 870 intersection that extended all the way to Route 864. An ideal secluded anchorage and possible site for a VC camp and cache of supplies coming down river from Cambodia. The footing was slippery. The slimy mud along the river was like gumbo. It sticks and becomes big clods of mud on each foot. It means that we need to stop and scrape the mud off our boots every few minutes and pick off the leeches that seemed to be everywhere. Last night's rain has stopped, but the trees are still dripping. Very slow going.

We made slow progress toward out target. My dead reckoning put us within about two hundred meters of the inlet. The heavy brush limited visibility. I was about to take a step when an Asian Cobra slithered over my left foot seeking cover away from the human invasion of its home ground. I am convinced that every poisonous snake in the world can be found here. Cobras, coral snakes, kraits and all kinds of vipers are here and most crawl around and over us. They seek the warmth from our bodies when we rest.

Our point man, White, raised his arm to signal us to halt. He was 10 meters ahead of me and pointed ahead to his right. I moved slowly and quietly up to him. I mentally thanked my dad for teaching me woodcraft, how to track wild game, and move stealthily in the bush. I knew that we were close and I carefully put down the toe of my boot setting down my foot quietly without snapping any twigs. Moving my body under branches that could move foliage and disclose our position.

I moved up beside White and immediately saw our target. The VC camp had 4 sampans tied up to the bank. There were no breakfast fires lit and I surmised that the inhabitants were still asleep after their night's work.

The navigable inlet ran 150 meters due north from the river and formed a nice little harbor away from the river's current. The water level was high and still rising from the torrential rain The plan of attack was straight forward. Guadanoli with his M60 would anchor this end of our firing line eliminating any potential river escape. I would sneak and peek my way north setting up squad members strategically on the perimeter with a clear kill zone, while I took the far end of the firing line.

Once I was in position the adrenaline high kicked in. My senses were on high alert and my eyesight focused. I had worked my way to 15 meters north of the last hootch. Well within range of my right arm. I double checked my weapons and then tossed a grenade into the hootch. I was a good, not great, fastball pitcher on my high school baseball team and this was a strike. The grenade exploded and it was fire at will.

Guadanoli cut loose with his M60 as several gooks broke for the river. Jones and Connell threw grenades into the other two hootches. Two shrapnel wounded gooks staggered out of the hootch in front of me. I dropped them each with a load of buckshot. White, Keane, and Rivera advanced to clear the hootches as we covered them.

It was over quickly.

We found a large ordnance cache beside the river. It was stored in an open sided thatch covered makeshift storage building. It contained boxes of 7.62x39mm ammo for AK-47's, boxes of 81 mm motor rounds, and a 75mm recoilless rifle, a copy of the US Model 20, that combined firepower and lightweight. We stacked the AK-47's that we found with the supplies and Jones wired a delay fuse to C4 plastic explosive to blow up the ordnance. We wanted to put some space between us and the explosion that would, for sure, bring in any NVA and VC in the immediate area.

We headed back along the river to meet our PBR for extraction. Some 20 minutes later when the weapons cache exploded, we had slip slided about a klick when the PBR nosed in to pick us up. Campbell, the PBR skipper, yelled hold on and stay low as he throttled up the twin diesels and boogeyed on out there. He said that he had received some incoming just down river and expected small arms fire from the shore.

Just as Campbell had warned as the boat picked up speed and got on plane a rocket skipped behind us and crashed into the trees on the other shore. We skimmed around a river bend at full throttle and incoming small arms fire buzzed around us like fatal bees. Several rounds plunked into the fiberglass port gunwale. The Gunner's Mate, Posey, opened up on the shoreline with the twin .50 calibers and a sailor named, Gratkowski, manned the aft 7.62mm machine gun on the port stern. The jungle foliage shook with the barrage, but no telling if it took out any of the gooks.

We sped away with no injuries. Just some gouges in the boat.

At 1430 I filed my after action report. Cmdr. Zanke had more work for us. The VC river pirates had interdicted shipping, capturing a South Vietnamese sampan loaded with market goods bound for My Tho. It had occurred in the Ben Tre Province just south of the Tien River confluence with the Mekong River. There was a floating market on the edge of the brown river water with a line of shanties and roughhewn wharfs where it was believed the VC river pirates were based. Swift boats (PDFs) regularly patrolled the river hoping to catch the VC pirates in the act. Our humane rules of engagement precluded just leveling the village and floating market which we might have accomplished with minimal opposition. So our job was to reconnoiter and determine if any returning sampans to the floating market were armed and had the spoils of river piracy. We would coordinate with the patrolling Swift boat and identify the VC pirate sampan for the brown water Navy. We would watch and stop any VC from escaping into the bush.

We had just enough time to clean our weapons, shower, and grab a couple hours of sleep. Jones took some time to cumshaw or borrow with the intent not to return a Stoner 63 machine gun which had a lot more punch than the M16 he had been carrying. His M16 was prone to jamming by failing to extract a fired cartridge. In the Rung Sat it was virtually impossible to keep the weapon clean and jams in a firefight were clearly to be avoided.

The Stoner was developed by Eugene Stoner and first produced in Costa Mesa, California. Later production moved to Warren, Michigan. It was a very effective gas operated, air cooled light machine gun that weighed about 12 pounds. The Stoner 63 chambered for the 5.56x45mm was fitted with a 150-round drum belt container the fed from the left side and the ejection port was closed with a dust cover to minimize dirt and gunk that could cause the action to jam.

We shipped out down river for our insertion point about 50 minutes away. The weather was nasty. Thunderstorms were rolling in and out. With every lightning bolt, I remembered that a boat was not where I should be in the middle of a thunder storm. We would be inserting at low tide which meant slogging through the mud, hopefully not under fire.

The thunder storm passed just before we reached our insertion point. We jumped over the bow of the PBR into a couple of inches of water and sunk another 4 inches in the ankle deep, sucking mud. Moving into the wet foliage seeking higher ground to walk on we stumbled onto a small dirt road. It was less muddy and we walked on the sides scanning the bush for any movement and the ground for any mines or booby traps. Staying off on side of the road so that we left few telltale boot tracks, we made good time.

We moved into the bush about a klick from the village and floating market. Moving as stealthily as possible, we took up positions to reconnoiter the sampan activity. Now came the hardest part of fulfilling our mission. We would quietly watch and wait. The sounds of the forest lulled us for the next 7 hours as we watched the relatively normal activities of the fishing boats come in with their catches of fish and eels. The brown, murky river water was surprisingly full of many species of fresh water and migratory fish, including giant cat fish that could approach 200 pounds. The villagers were cooking their evening meal as the next rain shower hit. We spent the night hunkered down under our ponchos as the village slept. There was no boat activity for the rest of the night.

The rain finally stopped in the chill before first light. The thick morning fog then developed and impaired our visual surveillance of the village and the anchored sampans. I was wet and uncomfortable. We couldn't smoke or move without potentially giving away our presence. About 0600 hours the village began to stir. We watched and waited. The villagers had their breakfast and performed their morning ablutions. The fog was beginning to lift as the sun rose higher.

We sat in the still dripping bush and watched. As the fisherman went out with their nets and trot lines, one of the larger junks with 4 gooks on board shoved off without any visible fishing equipment. It was a potential pirate boat headed down river toward mouth of the delta and the South China Sea.

We quietly crept back from the village. Getting out of hearing range, I called in the village position, a description of the pirate boat, and their direction. One of the PBF Swift boats would be hunting them this morning. We crept back into position to observe the village activities. We watched and waited. The activity increased dramatically at mid-day. The floating market was a beehive of activity. We watched as six armed gooks came ashore and went to one of the larger buildings. Soon other small groups of gooks began gathering by the building as one apparent leader stood outside speaking. It looked like a VC rally. I became convinced of it when they began handing out ammunition to the bystanders.

I signaled for the squad to drop back quietly. When I called in and relayed what we had found, I was told that our job was done and to go to the extraction point. The VC junk had been captured and an air strike would hit the village. Our job was done. Time for us to get out, get a shower, dry clothes, and some needed sleep.

On the long boat ride back to base, I felt a letdown that I had not experienced the adrenaline high of combat. The waiting and watching wasn't the same. My men were wet and tired, but unharmed. I should consider that success. In a few short months, I had made a transition. I don't know if it's mentally healthy to look forward to combat or rather the adrenaline high that comes with combat, but our good luck was holding and that should be enough. Everyone was quiet on the boat ride back to base. Maybe we were all becoming predators that looked forward to and fed off the adrenaline high of combat.

CHAPTER 8

Long Tau River

November 1965

The VC considered portions of the Rung Sat practically impenetrable by ground forces. There were VC on the Long Thanh Peninsula that were attacking cargo ships in the shipping channel to Saigon. Except for an occasional airstrike that might hit their camps or supply caches mostly by accident, they considered this a safe area. I had an intensive briefing on the Air Force's defoliation campaign that targeted the banks of the Long Tau River where several large VC camps and supply caches were known to be located. The Marines had a major operation in the planning stage to sweep the VC safe area in the Can Gio District and beyond.

We were in the transition period between the wet and dry seasons. The wet season was May to November and was characterized by heavy precipitation and high tides that reach 15 feet and flood the entire Run Sat.

Before the dry season that was just starting, it was important to get some ground reconnaissance. It was pretty clear that the Marines were planning a major operation before the end of the dry season. Operation Jackstay would commence in March or April. The VC encampments were usually on high ground where Nipa Palms grew. The trees could be picked out from aerial photographs. The Nipa Palm sap was used to make liquor, the fronds for thatch, and the seeds are edible. Nipa Palms grow where the ground was seldom flooded with the brackish tidal flow of the Mekong Delta. Although the soil was firm enough to walk on, in the rain it was sticky mud that would not support vehicle travel. The many streams had steep banks and could be up to 15 feet deep. The aerial photos of the insertion area showed a large grove of Nipa Palms northwest of the cleared area.

We would be inserted by helicopter and airlifted out after 48 hours, the amount of time for foot immersion or jungle rot to get established. Our insertion was delayed for a day as a line of violent thunder storms moved through.

Finally, the weather cleared. It was cloudy and 85 degrees with 80% relative humidity. I boarded the Huey Slick that would insert us and sat behind the door gunner. Unlike gunships, the Huey Slicks could transport six troops and had a pilot and door gunner with a mounted machine gun. Approaching the defoliated area on the west bank of the Long Tau River, the thick forest disappeared. It was a desolate blackened expanse. This area had been doused with agent orange and some areas napalmed to kill the foliage as a predecessor to Operation Jackstay.

The Slick or personnel transport helicopter dropped us off and immediately left. We fanned out and advanced west. There was no cover, just charred stumps. The soft, muddy earth gave up an odor of burned organic material with every step. It was slippery footing and I was very glad that there were no enemies hiding in the charred mess. The morning fog was beginning to dissipate. I felt like we were being completely revealed to any VC within a klick.

We cautiously had advanced due west about a kilometer when we came across the remains of a small village that had been burned. I counted 19 crispy critters. These had been VC caught in the napalm attack that had burned virtually everything down to the ground.

We had about 5 hours of daylight and I really wanted to get out of this charred devastation before stopping for a meal and some rest.

1530 hours and we are still slogging our way through the mess and we came upon a raging stream. It is only 3 meters across, but the current looks strong and the banks are almost vertical. Not worth trying to ford and no overhanging trees. No alternative except to follow the stream north.

Finally, we came to a crude foot bridge across the stream and there was green foliage on the other side. Carefully surveying the muddy ground leading to the foot bridge revealed no foot prints or recent traffic. Crossing quickly into the Nipa Palms on the far side I felt far less exposed and more comfortable in the bush.

There was a small foot trail leading west. Collins took the point and we moved silently forward through the Nipa Palm forest. The palm forest seemed devoid of wildlife. The little parakeets and ducks that were prevalent in the Rung Sat were nowhere around. I suspected that Agent Orange had killed everything. It was eerily quiet.

I whistled and signaled a stop. We needed rest and nourishment. There was a small rise and higher ground about 25 meters north of the foot trail. Our point man, Collins, led us there. Geary had the first watch and the rest of us spread our ponchos to have a dry spot to settle in for short rest.

Shortly after midnight under a full moon we saddled up and moved further west on the small trail. I knew the full moon would create a very high tide throughout the tidal estuary and we needed to stay on high ground. The Nipa Palm forest ran northwest of the mangroves and our anticipated extraction point was a small opening in the palms about 7 kilometers or about 4 miles west. We would reconnoiter the intervening high ground for enemy activity and encampments.

Bamboo grows virtually everywhere in Vietnam and is used for building, defense, sharpened stakes for booby traps, and the bamboo shoots for food. The sharpened stakes driven into the ground in a pit loosely covered with forest debris are referred to as Punji Sticks. Usually the stakes are dipped in feces to cause bacterial infection. While not usually fatal, the unfortunate victim suffers excruciating painful and bloody wounds.

Jones had the point. His right foot went through the dead palm fronds. He bent forward as he fell. One stake went through his right calf and another pierced his rib cage on the right side. SSgt. White was behind Jones and was the first to reach him. The big man reached down and lifted Jones out of the pit. The stakes were ripped out in the process. Jones was bleeding heavily and in great pain. Collins hurried up to him and injected morphine and applied an antiseptic agent. Then, he applied a compression bandage to his leg and wrapped his torso. Fortunately, the injury to his rib cage wasn't deep and had glanced off his rib cage, but a stake had gone right into his calf for about 2 inches.

I checked the map and aerial photos for possible nearby landing zones. We were in luck it looked like a small open area north of us. I sent Rivera and Keane ahead to reconnoiter as White and Geary volunteered to alternately carry Jones. I called in the coordinates to airlift Jones out.

It took us 25 minutes to reach the LZ. They must have scrambled the helicopter crew as soon as I called in because I could already hear the distinct whoop of the rotor as they came in for the dust off. So could the VC who were nearby.

When incoming rounds clipped the foliage around us, we hunkered down on the edge of the clearing as the Huey approached. "This is 1-4 we're hot. Repeat the LZ is hot."

I could see a shadow in the trees moving. I pumped three quick rounds of buckshot into the brush. Guadanoli was cutting down the brush at waist level with the M60 and the door gunner in the Huey opened up. White and Geary got Jones on board as the helicopter hovered. Without knowing the enemy strength, I ordered everyone to board and hoped the pilot could lift us off.

As we gained altitude, a large VC camp came into view just west of our extraction point. I noted the coordinates for my after action report. The Marines could follow up with an airstrike and neutralize this VC encampment.

At the end of the wet season, the 1st Battalion, 5th Marines would initiate Operation Jackstay with an amphibious assault on the Long Thanh peninsula. The objective of this large scale troop deployment was to clear the area of enemy activity.

I got word from Saigon that after cleaning his wounds and treating them for bacterial infection, Jones was going to be okay and likely would return to the platoon after about 4 weeks convalescence. He was very lucky that we were able to extract quickly. Punji Sticks could be fatal from hemorrhage and infection.

The Swift boat patrolling the My Tho River upstream to Cai Be about 50 kilometers from our My Tho Base had been getting small arms and rocket fire from the shore at several points. Reviewing the map with Lieutenant Junior Grade Ernest R. Walsh, the captain of PBF-33, it appeared that the incoming fire had been consistent around a bend in the river about 5 kilometers from Cai Be. It also appeared that there were at least two different VC groups operating since the incoming fire came from locations that were a couple of kilometers apart. Aerial reconnaissance had not shown any camps or villages close by, but the palm and bamboo forest was very thick.

We boarded the PBF for the next morning's patrol. Captain Walsh would drop us off before the we reached the first area where they had been fired upon. We would work our way west along the river and if the VC fired on the PBF this morning we should be able to find the perpetrators.

Capt. Walsh throttled down the 51-foot Swift boat and as quietly as possible eased in toward shore and dropped us off. We waded in shallow water to a sand bar. We checked our weapons and moved into the bush. The humidity was high and the there was still some morning fog over the water. Keane was on point and came across a foot trail paralleling the river. We moved in single file following the trail west. We had traveled only a few hundred meters when we heard the distinctive chatter of AK-47's up ahead followed by the PBF's .50 caliber machine guns answering. Then a significant blast that was probably a 40mm rocket fired from a Russian made shoulder mounted launcher.

We closed the distance between us and the VC on the river bank. The firefight was raging up ahead. I could see thick black smoke rising above the trees from the river. Another rocket blast.

Finally, we got close. The VC were so intent on sinking the PBF that our arrival went undetected. I could make out 5 gooks and signaled to spread out in a firing line. I called in our position to the PBF. Guadanoli took out the rocket launcher. The other 4 VC never knew what hit them. The Swift boat had been hit by two rockets and was belching black diesel smoke. There was visible damage to the bow.

The squad quickly searched the dead VC's for any documents that might be useful and threw their weapons into the river. LTJG Walsh was on the radio, "1-4 we have some damage and injuries. Our port engine is out, but we have put the fire. Suggest we pick you up there and we head back to My Tho for repairs. Our injuries are not life threatening. You?"

"We're good. Five dead gooks. No peanuts (injuries)."

The welded aluminum hull of the 50-foot Swift boat took most of the impact of the rocket. Capt. Walsh and his crew put out the fire, but one engine was out of commission. The Boatswain Mate, Miller, had a wounded left thigh. He that had a 3-inch laceration from some shrapnel. It was bloody, but not serious. It would get stitched up by one of the corpsmen at My Tho. The Engineman, Snyder, had a broken arm. An ugly compound fracture with white bone sticking out. They got his arm immobilized and in a sling, but he was still on the job babying the one remaining diesel engine to get us home.

The strong current helped us limp back to our My Tho base.

Capt. Walsh and I later met at mess that evening. His boat would be laid up for repairs for about a week. We assumed that there was another VC camp somewhere upriver on the opposite shore that had also been bothering river traffic. We both agreed that when his boat was repaired we would try a similar plan to neutralize that VC position.

CHAPTER 9

The Dry Season

December 1965

The last few weeks had been routine. It was wet season ended and the dry season with slightly cooler and drier weather was upon us. while it still rained occasionally, we were no longer experiencing wild thunder storms and heavy precipitation on a daily basis. Miraculously, Jones was recovering and his wounds were deemed non-critical for future service which meant that he might be back with the platoon after convalescence.

The dry season begins in December. The temperature moderates a little with less humidity in January and February is usually the driest month. I was hopeful that the jungle rot that I had on my feet and in my crotch would also dry up. I was applying some fungal lotion every day that the corpsman provided to us. We all had the problem from being wet and not being able to maintain the best hygiene. Dry socks were a luxury.

Cmdr. Zanke, Commander of SEAL forces in Vietnam, came to My Tho for a two-day meeting and inspection. What it meant for my platoon was two days in camp with an opportunity to perform maintenance on our weaponry, clothing, and most important find the right-sized boots to replace our rotting footwear.

A new offensive, Operation Game Warden, was described by Cmdr. Zanke. We would have a significant role along with the riverine units based here in My Tho, Bassac near the South China Sea, and in Tan Chau northwest on the Mekong River near Cambodia. I also was given some insight into policy concerns that seemed to me to be above my pay grade.

Marine Corps General Victor Krulak was expressing disagreement with General Westmoreland's strategy of attrition. It was "wasteful of American lives, promising a protracted, strength-sapping battle with small likelihood of a successful outcome." Krulak proposed instead a focus on a pacification program to provide village security plus increased air strikes. The concept of attrition as opposed to taking and holding territory and denying it's use to the enemy was hotly debated. Seizing territory and resources and thus denying them to the enemy was viewed by most military planners as the historical way to victory.

Operation Game Warden's objective was to deny the Viet Cong access to the resources of the Mekong Delta. U.S. Naval forces backed by Marine artillery on the ground would launch rapid surprise attacks on dozens of small Viet Cong ports scattered along the many rivers and tributaries in the delta.

Our job was straight forward. We would work in concert with River Division 53 based in My Tho. The boats would insert us to mop up the VC ports post-attack and capture and/or kill survivors.

One of the first attacks was an air strike on Ham Long southwest of My Tho. The F-4 Phantoms had reportedly destroyed the port and village with incendiary bombs and strafing runs with their M61 Vulcan 20mm Gatling cannons.

My platoon, short-handed with Jones on medical leave, would insert about a kilometer downstream from Ham Long. The plan was to approach the village undetected and eliminate any VC survivors and destroy any remaining food, medical, or ordnance caches.

I reported to Headquarters Company after breakfast with Guadanoli, Bravo Squad Leader, to review the aerial photos from yesterday's late afternoon airstrike. We discerned only 2 sampans still floating and 5 apparently undamaged hootches. The substantial buildings in Ham Long were either flattened or burning. There were visible bodies strewn on the ground. We figured there were some survivors and they would be busy salvaging what they could find this morning and would be on the alert for any intruders.

We boarded the PBR for an hour's boat ride upriver. The Patrol Boat's captain was a Navy Petty Officer named Campbell that had ferried us on several other missions. We knew each other and there was some mutual respect. He kept the PBR mid-stream as far from the river shore as possible to avoid or least make small arms fire difficult.

Right on schedule Campbell nosed the PBR into the river bank at our predetermined insertion point. So far so good. We would quietly cover the remaining kilometer or so to Ham Long.

White took the point on the small dirt road that led to Ham Long. We advanced along the road for 20 minutes until we were getting close, then began very slowly moving closer. White motioned for us to move off the road and he led 4 men into the bush on the right and I took the rest left. We did our sneak and peek to within 20 meters of the VC port and village.

There was some activity. I could see a wounded VC with a rifle sitting on a chair next to one of the remaining hootches. There were 2 young women gathering things from a demolished building near the wharf.

Dad had taught me early on that if there was going to be a fight, then hit your opponent first, knock him down, and don't let him up.

We had defensive positions 10 meters apart and opened fire on the visible Viet Cong survivors. There was limited return fire from the totally surprised remaining VC in the village. Rivera tossed a grenade into one of the remaining hootches and all enemy firing stopped.

Cautiously waiting and watching until I was certain that there was no additional movement, we moved building to building. Most were demolished from the airstrike. We burned the rest and threw the firearms into the river. Guadanoli turned his M60 on the sampans. He seemed to take joy in blasting them full of large holes.

We counted 27 dead gooks including women and children. Most were victims of the airstrike and were already covered with maggots and turning black and bloated.

Man, I need to change jobs.

We were an undersized platoon. SEAL platoons coming in-country now were comprised of 2 squads of 6-men (later they would be expanded again to 16 operators comprising 4 firing teams of 4-men each). We were really 2 fire teams of 4-men each plus me.

As Operation Game Warden was gaining momentum, we had regular follow up missions mopping up small encampments and doing the attack post-mortems. It was pretty morbid duty that consisted mostly of counting crispy critters or the burned and often dismembered bodies of the VC's caught in the airstrike or artillery barrage that preceded our arrival.

The NVA and VC had used hit and run tactics up until last month when they had met head on with U.S. and South Vietnamese forces in the Battle of Ia Drang north of the Rung Sat Special Zone. The North Vietnamese suffered heavy casualties. The Air Force had been bombing the North since March, but President Lyndon Johnson ordered a halt to Operation Rolling Thunder this month. He then undertook negotiations with North Vietnam. These efforts were frustrated for many reasons, but the North Vietnamese believed that politics in the domestic U.S. would not permit the U.S. to utilize its military and economic power in South Vietnam.

While the NVA leadership listened to the U.S. media and some movie star sympathizers, we just wanted to do our job, survive our tour of duty, and return home with ten fingers and toes.

I tried not to listen or believe what was in the occasional news cast that was viewed at the base Officers' Club on the rare evenings when I was on base. We had never lost a firefight and were feared in the swamp, yet Hollywood and the news made us out to be losers. Everyone in my platoon had volunteered and the media said it was only the poor who got drafted to serve in 'Nam. I understood that we were here to defend the freedom and independence of South Vietnam and our country was obligated by the Geneva Accords. I didn't understand the blame being directed at us.

CHAPTER 10

Quang Tri

January 1966

Cmdr. Zanke invited (ordered) me to attend a meeting with Marine Corps General Walt. The 5th Marines were planning a major campaign in the Central Highlands. The CIA had a continuing role with the Phoenix Program and I was introduced to a CIA operative named, De Silva. He was in charge of the operation out of Saigon. The High Rice Plains ran north to the Annamese Cordillera Mountains and west to the mountains bordering Cambodia. This was assumed to be one of the major supply routes from the North and through Cambodia for the VC operating in the Mekong Delta. It later was determined that most supplies came down the Mekong River system.

The Annamese Cordillera Mountain chain runs parallel to the Vietnamese coast in a gentle curve which divides the basin of the Mekong Delta from Vietnam's narrow coastal plain along the South China Sea. The heavily wooded mountains rise steeply about 3000 feet. Most of the crests are on the Laotian side and Northeastern Cambodia. It is moist broadleaf rain forest. The eastern slope was populated by ethnic minorities that the French had left largely to their own animistic devices. The French had indentured them occasionally to work on their tea, coffee, pepper, and rubber plantations. They were sometimes forcibly enrolled as mercenaries to guard against the anti-colonial Vietminh. This anti-colonial sentiment was still strong.

It became evident that the SEALs would be the forward eyes and ears for the 5th Marines campaign. We needed to change our thinking and strategy from the swamp we had been operating in to the heavily forested high country. And we had to say good bye to our boat rides.

My squad leader, Joe Guadanoli, Chief Petty Officer, had become the steady and reliable right hand man that was always there when I needed him. He had the team ready to saddle up with extra ammo and full 70 pound packs to sustain us for an extended mission. We flew out on two Huey slicks. Our insertion point was in the strategic Quang Tri Valley some 120 kilometers northwest. The valley runs from the mountains eastward toward the seacoast. For weeks intelligence had reported that NVA troops and supplies were filtering down the Ho Chi Minh Trail into the Quang Tri Valley. Our job was to reconnoiter, capture for interrogation, and verify targets with specific coordinates before the major campaign began. Also, there was intelligence that the North Vietnamese General Hoan Nguyen Giap was somewhere in the area. Giap reported directly to General Tran Van Tra the NVA General who led the war in the field against us. There was a Marine sniper in the area looking to terminate Giap and we should assist only if necessary. In other words, don't get in his way.

There was a large Marine base in Khe Sanh down the valley. We heard that some 5,000 Marines would be moving up the valley. Our efforts would be critical for the Battle for Ia Drang Valley that would follow our mission.

GySgt. Rose with the 3rd Marines had given me advice on the terrain that was ahead of us. Close cover that was heavily wooded and brush covered meant close quarters. The open rice plains could be covered with the platoons M60's, M14's, and M16's, but when in the bush it would be close quarters with target visibility of maybe 10 meters. I took his advice. I had carried a shotgun since August and I managed to cumshaw (borrow with no intent to return) another Ithaca Model 37 militarized 12-gauge shotgun with an extended tubular feed for Collins, my Radioman and all the buckshot that I could carry. I could hold the trigger back and pump it as fast as I could to create a lead wall of .33 caliber pellets that would cut down trees or cut a gook in half.

The Ithaca Model 37 had the fewest parts of any pump shotgun at the time. It is easily used either right or left handed because, unlike most other pump shotguns, it loads and ejects through the bottom of the weapon's receiver. Marine Corps Armorers had extended the tubular feed to almost the length of the 20-inch barrel to accommodate 8 shotgun shells. The barrel is attached to the receiver by an interrupted thread. It is easily removed for cleaning by unscrewing the knurled plug on the end of the magazine tube, turning it 90 degrees, and pulling it off the receiver. Cleaning a plugged barrel quickly and easily in combat conditions can be significant. The Model 37 can put 72 pellets of 00 buckshot (.33 caliber) down range as fast as the forearm can be cycled. Once the trigger is pulled for the first shot, the disconnector allows the gun to fire all the ammunition in its magazine by merely cycling the forearm. In this regard, it puts your average submachine gun to shame. The only disadvantage is that shotgun shells are big and bulky.

The LZ was thankfully quiet as we disembarked from the Hueys. Jones was still on medical leave. My platoon was down to nine men.

It included Guadanoli, Joseph, Chief Petty Officer, USN, Collins, Mitchell R. PO-1 USN, Geary, Joseph L. CPO-3 USN, Connell, John L. PO-2 USN, Rivera, Jose J. PO-2, USN, White, Richard F, SSgt USMC, Keane, Earl K., PO-2 USN, Jaros, Joseph K, PO-2 USN, and Castanaro, George E, PO-1 USN. All but Guadanoli, and Collins had gone through BUD/s with me. We had bonded. Chief Guadanoli and Petty Officer Collins had already served a tour of duty as advisors to the ARVN Rangers teaching guerilla tactics.

The ridge about 5 kilometers north of us was indicated as a likely transition point where the Ho Chi Minh Trail branched off east toward the Drang Valley. I knew to stay off the trails leading up the mountain because they most likely would be booby trapped with trip wires, Punji sticks dipped in feces, and land mines.

Guadanoli took the point as we indianed our way up staying 5 meters apart. He didn't go far into the trees before he put his hand up for us to stop. There was noise ahead and to our right. We crouched in anticipation. Three wild pigs burst out of the cover and raced downhill. Fortunately, no one gave away our position with a jumpy trigger finger. Something or someone up ahead had flushed those pigs.

I whispered to my RM (Radio Man) Collins for the team to take a defensive position on the high ground looking down on the trail and wait. He passed it along and the team quietly moved into position near the trail. We covered about 35 meters of the trail and had a clear kill zone. Guadanoli held the north point of the firing line with his M60. He would wait until the enemy got into our kill zone before he opened up with full automatic fire.

We were about 5 meters above the trail hidden in the bush. I could barely detect some stealthy movement coming down the trail. They must have detected our insertion. The two bladed Huey helicopters make a distinct sound and were probably visible pulling up if the gooks were on this first ridge. Here they come.

The gooks were in NVA uniforms. They were slowly searching each side of the trail. I counted 19 gooks on the south side of the trail and there were more on the north side or about a full infantry platoon-size unit coming at us. Hopefully, we were concealed well enough to let them pass into the kill zone. As the last man in line approached his position Guadanoli opened fire and that was the signal for fire at will. The center of the gook platoon was shielded by dome low vegetation and some of the NVA survived the opening fire of our ambush by diving into the brush. The staccato chatter of AK-47's sent rounds whizzing by us and chipping bark off the trees. My face was stung by some wood chips.

A gook was firing from a prone position about 10 meters away behind a low wall of brush at trail side. I pumped two rounds of buckshot into the brush in front of him. His hands flopped above the brush as he was blown backwards. Thank you, Gunny, shotguns are devastating at close range.

We heard the sound of several gooks scrambling up the hill away from us. The firefight was over in less than 4 minutes. Everyone checked in OK. We had counted coup as my ancestors had in the American West years ago. There were 17 dead gooks and two wounded badly that we dispatched. I counted four more blood trails going up the hill with the survivors. We searched the bodies for any useful intelligence material, but this was just a patrol sent out to get us.

Calling in to Battalion HQ, I reported our action. Major Hornady, the Battalion XO, told me that intel pinpointed a company sized encampment on the ridge above us and another battalion sized encampment about 5 klicks further north. The Marine sniper was expected to be somewhere north of us attempting to get at a shot at General Giap at the larger encampment.

We saddled up to get a better look at the top of the ridge.

It was slow going uphill in heavy vegetation and we had to be quiet. White was on point. It still surprised me how a big African-American weighing some 250 pounds in shape could move so quietly. I had made him an honorary member of my Shoshoni tribe and my blood brother. The sweat was pouring off me. I noticed a large dark blood stain on Guadanoli's left shoulder and arm.

I whistled and motioned to him. Guadanoli came over and said, "it's superficial, Lt, I caught a stinger in the fire fight."

He had a deep 3-inch laceration that was bleeding a lot. I helped him wrap it tightly to compress the wound. He reinforced that he was OK and ready to move out. I was breathing hard when we crested the ridge and I called for a quick break.

At about 2200 feet above sea level on the crest of the hill our visibility was limited. The forest canopy virtually shut out the sun. Guadanoli was jumping around. The fallen log that he sat on was rotten and home to voracious, biting ants. They were worse than the leeches in the swamp. Time to move out again.

We did a sneak and peek along the top of the ridge. White was on point again and his hand went up to signal us to stop. We were on high alert. Some distant voices could be barely heard. The gook camp was situated in a high meadow. White reported back that about 200 gooks were camped ahead of us and they had at least two mortars. I motioned to Collins to come over and called in the coordinates.

Our job was done for now. It looked like there was a possible opening for our extraction about 3 klicks southwest and White was again on point as we quietly disappeared in the bush and went down from the ridge.

The tough conditions slowed our descent and it was 1730 hours when we arrived at our extraction point. It was a good LZ for our extraction and I called in the coordinates and confirmed our position. I was ordered to overnight and assume defensive positions. Apparently, the air strike starting with the ridge top gook encampment was about to begin. I guessed that the sound or sight of helicopters could be the wrong signal. It wasn't long before we could see and hear Puff the Magic Dragon unloading on the ridge top.

Puff the Magic Dragon was the nickname for the Douglas AC-47D Spooky gunship (the military version of the DC-3). It had been modified by mounting three MXU-470/A guns to fire through two rear window openings and the side cargo door, all on the left (pilot's) side of the aircraft.

The guns were actuated by a control on the pilot's yoke, where he could control the guns either individually or together, although gunners were also among the crew to assist with gun failures and similar issues. Spooky's primary function was close air support for ground troops. It could orbit the target for hours. Coverage given by a Spooky was over an elliptical area approximately 47 meters in diameter, placing a round every 2.2 meters during a 3-second burst. Each of its three 7.62 mm mini guns could selectively fire either 50 or 100 rounds per second. Cruising in an overhead left-hand orbit at 120 knots air speed at an altitude of 3,000 feet the gunship could put a bullet or glowing red tracer bullet (every fifth round) into every square yard of a football field-sized target in potentially less than 10 seconds. The aircraft also carried flares, which it could drop to illuminate the battleground. Puff the Magic Dragon was airborne devastation to ground troops.

HQ was using Puff to be more surgical than bombs to give the Marine sniper a chance to exit successfully.

Our extraction the following morning was uneventful. We heard later the Marine sniper was successful in terminating General Giap and had literally crawled through the brush for three days with his spotter as the gooks hunted him. The sniper, Sgt. Carlos Hathcock, was becoming a Marine Corps legend.

The Marines needed our assistance to reconnoiter and disrupt the supply lines leading to the Ia Drang Valley. Mostly, they wanted an NVA officer captured for intelligence. The CIA used very effective interrogation techniques that had consistently provided us with good intelligence.

Friday, we had been airlifted to a position near the Laotian border. There was a large NVA/VC compound on the Laos side. Our job was to interdict the supply line coming into South Vietnam and, hopefully, capture one or more NVA for interrogation. We found a small road leading towards the Bolaven Plateau. Inside of the South Vietnamese border, we set up to wait for and observe any traffic coming from Laos. We were in a largely unpopulated area. The hours went by and we became accustomed to the sounds of the surrounding forest. The critters here were very different from the swamp. There were antelope-like Saola and the Indochinese Tiger.

Sunday morning at 0930 hours there was movement on the road. There was a squad-size unit in NVA uniforms coming down the single lane track. Carefully studying the NVA soldiers, I could identify an officer walking in front. From our position, we had a clear kill zone at a range of about 20 meters.

My mind went back to deer hunting with my dad. Waiting on a stand to ambush a buck coming down the mountain to feed. Come on Jack – focus. I can't let my mind wander or someone may get hurt because of me. The NVA squad is in our kill zone. They have no chance of escape. I shot the lead NVA officer in the legs. We wanted him alive.

Like most of our firefights, surprise and positioning were key elements for superiority. It was over quickly. We had Huey Slicks (personnel helicopters) on stand-by so we would transport the wounded, this time, for the CIA to interrogate. I called for extraction and was anxious for us to transported out before a larger enemy force found us. The CIA had 3 wounded NVA including an officer to cross-exam.

We spent the days leading up to the Marines campaign interdicting and destroying the VC supply caches and booby trapping their supply lines.

CHAPTER 11

The Rung Sat

February 1966

The driest month in South Vietnam is usually February. The first week in February, we were ordered back to the riverside base in My Tho. Our three weeks in the central highlands had been nasty. Guadanoli got hit in the left shoulder and had been stitched up by a corpsman at the Marine Base. His flak jacket took the brunt of the it, but his left shoulder had a deep laceration and the stitches had just been removed.

The VC had established several camps in the swamp south of My Tho. They used these for rest and re-supply for their forays into the surrounding villages. Village chieftains were summarily executed if they did not comply with the VC demands for food and recruits. While the Army and Marine Corp patrols would cover the surrounding villages, our job was to root them out of the Rung Sat swamp.

The PBR (Patrol Boat River) carried us down river to our jumping off spot and would be on-call to extract us with 2 hours notice. The

Rung Sat Special Zone comprised about 1200 square kilometers (485 square miles) of tidal mangrove swamp including some 4,800 kilometers if interlocking streams and canals south of Saigon.

This area was critical to the security of the Long Tau River, main shipping channel from Saigon to Vung Tau. The Viet Cong established base areas in the zone and ground operations were extremely difficult. In 1965, the USAF had begun defoliating the area as part of Operation Ranch Hand, but attacks on allied shipping had been increasing.

The tidal marsh and mangrove roots made foot travel slow, hard work. The mosquitoes and blood sucking leeches in the stagnant, foul-smelling water were unbearable. I began dreaming about the central highlands that we had just left behind us. After five hours were had traveled less than 2 kilometers in the mangrove swamp. Our intelligence indicated a large supply cache somewhere in the area.

Finding a dry island in the swamp at 1400 hours, I believed that we were close to the camp and that was quickly verified as I smelled smoke. Guadanoli had his hand up signaling us to stop. With Collins on my heels I creeped up to him. The gook cook was barbequing a pig for the night's feast. There was no other movement in the camp. I suspected that the gooks were asleep or resting up for their evening raid. It looked like there was a navigable tributary on the far side of the camp. If there were sentries on duty, that's the probable spot.

Planning our attack, I motioned the team to my position. Guadanoli with his M60 and White would crawl over to the west side blocking any down river escape and take out any sentries by the river. Collins and I would position ourselves up river. Geary, Connell, Rivera, and Castanaro would be spread out in the center. Since Collins and I had the farthest to go, we would initiate the attack.

I led Collins on a circle route upriver. The vile, stinking water was thigh deep and the mosquitoes were drinking our blood. The high ground that we skirted covered about five acres. The VC had built semi-permanent hootches. They obviously thought this was a safe supply base for incursions into the villages north and to harass and interdict shipping. We crawled up on dry land with some low brush and reeds providing cover. I had to chuckle when I noticed that one of the VC boats was powered by a battered Mercury outboard motor made in Wisconsin.

Collins whispered, "Last hootch on the left."

A gook was coming out and stretching about 35 meters away. Carrying an AR-16 with a 30 round clip. I switched to full automatic fire and triggered a three shop tap. When I shot him the team opened up spraying the hootches and lobbing in grenades.

We had stirred up a hornet's nest. Gooks were charging out of their hootches firing their AK-47's at the perimeter. We were entrenched and much better shots. Keane and Jaros crawled to the edge of the bush and tossed grenades into the sampans discouraging any escape by river. The devastating fire that we trained on the camp caught the VC completely by surprise. We quickly ran out of targets and lobbed grenades into the remaining hootches that were still standing.

As I was calling in, Geary came up and told me that there were 23 dead gooks and 2 badly wounded that would not survive. We had two minor scratches. Castanaro got a lacerated left arm from a hot piece of shrapnel and Connell broke his thumb when he hit the deck. We were lucky and beginning to feel 10 feet tall and bullet proof. A dangerous attitude in-country that could get us killed.

Extraction was scheduled for 1830 hours about 2 klicks upriver. I called in to confirm our extraction and move it to our current location since it was pacified. We torched the supply caches, hooches, and blew up the boats. Covering even a couple of kilometers to meet our scheduled extraction would be difficult in this terrain.

With 10 minutes to spare for our scheduled extraction, I called for a leech check. I never really enjoyed smoking, but I lit a cigarette to burn off the leeches. Man, I hate the little bastards. As I pulled up my soggy fatigue pants, I heard the PBR approach.

"Saddle up, our ride home is here," I said to the team.

The 31 foot PBR with a shallow two-foot draft and jet drives easily made it to our position on the muddy river bank. Tired, dirty, and anxious to get out of the swamp, we loaded up. The Chief Petty Officer who captained the boat, said that he had seen the smoke from where we burned the VC supply depot 2 klicks downriver and was concerned that other VC in the area also saw it.

Sure enough the whomp of a B-40 rocket as the projectile took out the starboard aft gunwale and continued through the port gunwale. A second B-40 missed and skipped across the water. It hit the trees and the backlash sprayed us with shrapnel and splinters. Chief Porter jammed the throttles forward and got up on plane in a hurry. We raced away up river at close to thirty knots.

The damage to the boat was fortunately above the water line. The force of the explosion had lifted me off the deck. One of the boat crew, a sailor named Homan, had a leg sheared right off above the knee. Castanaro had shrapnel embedded in his right thigh. Collins had been at my side and had been mostly shielded from the shrapnel by my body, but his broken thumb was at a weird angle and he was bleeding from a laceration to his right thigh. I was bleeding from a neck laceration and both arms were punctured by shrapnel. My torso was protected by my flak jacket. In shock, I felt no pain, but I knew that would catch up to me.

The boat captain, Chief Porter, headed home at full throttle and called in. There was a corpsman waiting at the dock and an airlift waiting to take us to the hospital in Saigon when we arrived at the base camp. The sailor, Homan, was carried on to the helicopter first. Castanaro, Collins, and I jumped in behind the stretcher The corpsman administered lifesaving emergency first aid to Homan binding up his bleeding stump and checking the tourniquet that had been put on him on the boat. Castanaro, Collins, and I were bleeding a lot, but we were not critical. Connell would get his thumb set and stayed with the platoon. The corpsman wrapped my bleeding arms, put a compression bandage on my neck over the right side of my collar bone, and shot me full of morphine. Good stuff. I floated the rest of the way to Saigon in my own little world.

I woke up in a hospital ward filled with wounded. It was clean and air conditioned. A pretty Navy nurse came by and introduced herself as Rebecca. She said that I would be fine and that I was stitched up and ready to be released by tomorrow. After a good night's sleep, I self-assessed my wounds as superficial. I had three shrapnel wounds in my left arm and two in my right. A deep laceration on my right shoulder below my neck had been cleaned out and stitched. The medication had worn off and everything ached, but I was alive and okay. Rebecca, the nurse, came by to tell me that they needed my bed and handed me a 10-day supply of Tramadol to ease the pain. I was released on 10-day medical leave. I was to report back in 10 days to have the stitches out and get a final medical review before being released for return to duty.

Homan, the sailor whose leg was blown off, had been stabilized and then flown to Hawaii. Castanaro and Collins had been released on medical leave yesterday. I hitched a helicopter ride back to My Tho. I could be useful at the base until the stitches were pulled out. The corpsman could easily do that in My Tho when the wounds had healed next week.

CHAPTER 12

Short-Timer

March 1966

Collins and Castanaro were back after some medical R&R to let their wounds heal. Once the stitches were out, we were all deemed medically fit for action. Connell's broken thumb was still splinted and taped, but he was back with the platoon. We now had a new SEAL commander, Lt. Commander Arthur L. Walsh. Our command structure still went through the Special Operations Command and Cmdr. Zanke, in charge of riverine activities, but we had one of our own calling the shots right above us in country and local. We looked at this very favorably since one of our own would be determining where we could best use our training.

For the record, there were less than 200 SEALs that served in Vietnam and they conducted 153 missions with only one man killed in action in their first year of operation. By the end of the conflict they accounted for some 580 Vietcong killed by confirmed body count, hundreds more probable kills, and over a thousand prisoners. The VC kept meticulous handwritten records, maps of the trails, and the river system, including all the little tributaries. We found their commo-liaison routes from their own maps that we captured. Of course, we then set booby traps along their routes.

Operation Jackstay was launched. The 1st Battalion 5th Marines and two Battalions of Vietnamese Marines began a search and clear mission along the Long Tau shipping channel that we had scouted a couple of months ago. They killed 63 VC and destroyed large supply caches. Following conclusion of Operation Jackstay security for the zone was passed to the Mobile Riverine Force.

The VC and some sympathizers had hit a village southwest of Ben Tre. The Marines Chieu Hoi (Vietnamese interpreter/interrogator) had gained information from the villagers that the VC camp was about 2 kilometers up a small tributary that flowed into the Mekong River. Chieu Hoi translates to Open Arms and it was a PsyOps Program that provided amnesty to captured VC and NVA. The Chieu Hoi proved to be brutal extractors of information from VC captives.

Based on the info that the Chieu Hoi had extracted from a captured VC, I planned a night time sweep to destroy a VC encampment that was indicated to be on a tributary upriver. We got the go ahead from Naval Support Ops and I briefed the platoon.

As the shadows were growing long, we inserted at the mouth of the tributary. We would follow the small river upstream and hopefully find the VC camp. If we came upon Highway 60 about 5 klicks up stream, then we had missed it or the info was bad. We had a long slog in the dark and sure enough we came out on Highway 60. Bad info. We sat by the bridge. I called for extraction. The PBR would take about an hour to reach us. The critters in the brush began rustling around in the bewitching pre-dawn darkness. It had been a long, fruitless walk in the dark.

My report identified the VC turncoat Chieu Hoi. The Marines and the CIA operatives would have to deal with him. I did not want to risk my platoon on any intelligence from him again. It had been a hard, long slog through nasty conditions. The VC had been tipped off that we were coming or they were never there.

Two days later, I took Alpha Squad to reconnoiter the Ben Tre village that was sympathetic with the VC. At the start of the war, the VC had attacked the province capitol and had temporary control of Ben Tre Province that had been previously been called Kien Hoa Province. The Viet Cong set up committees and confiscated land. The female VC leader, Madame Nguyen Thi Dinh, led an all-female "Long Hair Army". She was the secretary of the Communist party and a Major General in the army.

The Province is between two main branches of the Tien Giang River. The entire province is crisscrossed with tributaries creating an extensive irrigation system for the rice fields that dominate the province. The province is about 896 square miles and is on average only about 4 feet above sea level. Consequently, operations need to be conducted during the dry season before the torrential rains that can flood most of the land area.

We inserted about a klick away from the village and purposely avoided the road to remain covert. Timing our approach to the village for the late evening hours, we took up positions to observe the village as it came to life after dawn. I had learned to stay far enough away so that the ever present village dogs would not sound an alert. We carefully selected positions and settled in to watch and wait. We waited quietly. About 0200 hours we observed 4 gooks, a mortar squad, slip back into the village. We waited some more. As the birds and critters began their pre-dawn chattering, the village slowly came to life. The villagers came out their hootches and began their morning routines.

The breakfast fires were started. We watched the rather routine activities for an hour and a half. Five young men then came together each carrying AK-47's. They were VC fighters that had come home for the night to see wives, families, and girlfriends. The mortar squad was the night shift and these guys were the day shift.

Alpha Squad opened fire. It was overwhelming and concentrated on the five VC standing together. They were dead or dying in less than 25 seconds. We then concentrated fire on the hootches where the mortar squad had gone. There was no returned fire from the village. Alpha Squad quietly left the area. The psychological effect of the Green Faces ambush would make the village less enthusiastic to support the VC.

We were down to zero remaining days in-country. I wanted to get my men out quickly and safely. I called for extraction at our insertion point. I estimated that by the time we reached it, a PBR could be just arriving to pick us up. We took the road back and the boat was just slowing down to idle into the river bank as we arrived. I was thankful to whatever gods maybe. My squad was unscathed in our last action before going home.

CHAPTER 13

Back to the States

March 1966

We were in our seventh month in Vietnam. The VC called us Green Faces and put a bounty on our heads. The powers that be allowed us to stay in country for only 180 days or half the Army and Marine Corps one-year deployment. My platoon had over-stayed. We got back to My Tho in time for a late breakfast and we received orders for the platoon to rotate back to the states.

Two days later my platoon was back at Coronado, the West coast SEAL base. I had a 30-day leave and decided to go home and see my parents. There are no commercial flights from San Diego to Pinedale, Wyoming. I decided to fly commercial from San Diego to Salt Lake City, then take a bus to Pinedale, Wyoming.

It was a huge mistake to go in uniform. I had heard about the misinformed college kids that disagreed with our country's decision to live up to our treaty for defense. I was totally unprepared for the hate and shouted epithets. The bearded young man and his girlfriend were screaming at me as I entered the terminal at the San Diego airport. I barely kept my cool and remembered that I was home. Some heroes homecoming. The news on TV last night sounded as if we were losing. My platoon never lost a fight. The hurt would stay with me for a long time. I wondered what it would be like at home.

It had been eight years since I left for college in Austin, Texas. While in school at the University of Texas, my summers consisted of a Midshipman's cruise and football practice.

Pinedale is on the edge of the Wind River Mountain range. The high country is still wild and free. Dad was always up there guiding for elk or mule deer in the fall and fishing the headwaters of the Green River in the spring. During World War II, his amazing eye sight got him into flight school. After 12 missions in the European Theater, Dad was rotated stateside and became an IP or Instructor Pilot at Love Field in Dallas, Texas. A week after the Armistice, he was back in his beloved mountains doing what he loved best in the high country.

As his first born, Dad doted on me and introduced me to the wild country that he loved. I followed his pointy-toed boots everywhere. The woodcraft skills that he taught helped me stay alive in Southeast Asia. Growing up hunting and fishing imbued me with a love of the wild country. Dad taught me the survival skills and the marksmanship that my military instructors praised and won top honors in training.

The Museum of the Mountain Men in Pinedale chronicled the history of the fabled Green River Rendezvous in Jim Bridger's days. Dad was a descendent of Ernest (Big Ernie) Stryker, a trapper who came down from Canada and a Shoshone maiden, my great-grandparents. Mom was the daughter of Helen Howe from Boston and Irving Seymour, an English and Seneca Indian first generation American.

I loved my parents dearly, but by urban standards they were dirt poor and lower middle class. Dad is held in great esteem as a hunter and tracker, but those skills didn't translate easily to a paying job. He does some guiding for the sports who come out from the city. He calls them pilgrims. Within hours, the pilgrims invariably trust Dad in the wilderness and follow his pointy-toed footprints miles from civilization. From the time I could walk, I followed those scuffed cowboy boots hunting the Wind River Range and the Bridger-Teton National Forest just west of us. Sometimes not even hunting, but just out for the splendor of it all. Football and elk season conflicted. I always my shot my elk, but Dad didn't get to see many games. My first paying job as a high school sophomore was in the rental shop at the ski resort with unlimited free skiing as a perquisite. Meeting people from all over the map at the resort that winter really gave me a different perspective. I seriously thought about college and wondered how I could ever afford it. Football, good grades, and SATs over 1200 helped, but the Navy's NROTC program made it possible. They paid tuition and $75. per month. Head Coach and Athletic Director Darrell Royal kicked in some room, board, and books as long as I made the team.

When the bus pulled into Pinedale, downtown looked unchanged. I was grateful that no protesters were there. I met Joey on my first walk downtown. Joey and I played baseball together from Little League to American Legion summer ball. Joey was our high school ace pitcher. The strike out king and hero of the Regional American Legion baseball playoffs. Joey was drunk at 4:00 in the afternoon. Joey worked for the highway department and got off work at 3:00 pm. It only got worse.

I wandered over to the Pinedale Pub, the local watering hole. Several of my high school buddies and former team mates were there.

Alan Alves was a fireman. Donnie Eagle worked for the highway department with Joey. I got a rousing welcome and they called me "sailor boy". Alan quickly brought up that touchdown pass that I threw to him to win the Thanksgiving game. Jimmy Hatcher, the big center on my high school football team, joined us. Jimmy was in uniform and still on duty as one of Pinedale's three police officers. He had already heard that I was back and stopped in to say hello.

Two beers later, I excused myself from reliving our high school years and walked home. It was good to be home, but the highlight of my friends lives to date had been their high school years. Jimmy Hatcher had been to California for Basic Training in the Marine Corps Reserve, but washed out with a bad knee. The other guys had barely, if ever, been out of Sublette County, Wyoming.

Spring in the high country is a wonderful time of the year. The melting snow fills the streams. The elk and mule deer finally have a food surplus. The grouse are drumming in the trees. Dad convinced me to hike back in mountains with him to catch some trout and decompress. He never asked about things in Vietnam. He knew better. He rarely mentioned his military experience. I enjoyed the trip and Dad's quiet strength that exuded his being. We caught trout on wet flies just below the surface and on streamers in the fast water. It was a rejuvenation, but my leave was growing short and I wanted to fly to Austin and check in with the Herndon's on my way back.

It was a good visit with Mom and Dad, but Pinedale hadn't changed. It was depressing to think about my high school buddies and their future. They were mostly married to pretty girls that had become fat wives with several children. There were very limited opportunities in Pinedale and I missed my SEAL team. Guys that I knew I could depend on under duress. In civilian life you're lucky to have five real friends that you can depend on. In the military that group is more like twenty and it gets larger the longer that you serve.

When I called the Herndon's in Austin, Texas, their housekeeper told me that they were in New York for Carole's wedding. Surprised and more than little heart-broken I hung up and took the bus to Salt Lake City for my trip back to Coronado.

C H A P T E R 1 4

Coronado

April 1966

Reunited with my team at the SEAL base on Coronado Island next to San Diego, I felt like I was home. Jones was back with the platoon from medical leave. We did some serious physical training to get in shape for our next deployment. The guys were rested and mentally ready to go back into the action and count coup.

I received a letter from Tommy's Dad.

> *Dear Jack,*
>
> *Sue and I are very sorry that we missed you. As you know, Carole married Phil Conners in New York City last month. You will like Phil when you meet him. He's a pediatrician and they are living in White Plains, New York just outside of the city. They are a very happy young couple.*
>
> *We are glad that you are back stateside and look forward to seeing you at the ranch whenever you can make it.*

> *Tommy has been deployed with the 5th Marines and we think that he is based south of Saigon at a Marine base near the Mekong Delta. His promotion to 1st Lieutenant came through last month and he is the platoon leader for Delta Company, 3rd Platoon. You may run into him if and when you ship back over there.*
>
> *Stay safe. Our thoughts and prayers are with you and Tommy.*
>
> *Chet Herndon*

Cmdr. Kaufman, in charge of SEAL Training Depot, Coronado, ordered me to Camp Pendleton just up the road with a note that the uniform of the day would be Tropical Dress Long, the starched white choke collar that like most naval officers I hated. I arrived a proper five minutes early and was escorted by a GySgt. Jenner to the parade ground. The Gunny informed me that a proper award ceremony was planned with all the pomp and circumstance that the Navy and Marine Corps could muster.

I was escorted to a group of seats on the right hand side of the podium that had been set up on a small platform. There were three Marines and me seated on the right. Brigadier General Forrest Taylor, USMC, Colonel David Mehrfeldt, USMC, and Commander Richard Kaufman, USN, were seated behind the podium. The parade band and a full company of Marines marched by in front of us. The order to halt was barked followed by a left face, and parade rest.

After The General's introductory comments, the Colonel read the exploits of 1st Lt. Joseph S. Morganelli who received the Bronze Star for heroic action in Chou Lai with the 1st Marines. SSgt. William D. Storms was presented the Navy/Marine Distinguished Service

Medal. Corporal David M. Antonelli was presented the Navy/ Marine Distinguished Service Medal.

Then, it was Cdr. Kaufman's turn to introduce Stryker, Jack NMN (No Middle Name), Lt., USNR. He gave a succinct summary of action in the Rung Sat and I was presented with the Navy/Marine Distinguished Service Medal and a Bronze Star with a V for valor in combat. It would go into my sea bag along with my Purple Heart, Defense Meritorious Service Medal, Navy/Marine Corps Commendation Medal, and Vietnam Service Medal.

Still feeling ten feet tall and bullet proof, I was ready to go back in-country.

I received overnight liberty for getting the Bronze Star and Distinguished Service Medal. Returning to Coronado to change into civilian clothes, I ran into Joe Guadanoli and Mitch Collins. I invited them to join me for a celebratory drink in San Diego Old Town. We piled into my turquois and white 1956 Mercury Monterey and crossed the bridge to San Diego. Commandeering a table outside of the Matador, a Mexican restaurant in Old Town, we and ordered Margaritas.

Good enchiladas, the strolling Mariachi band, and several pitchers of Margaritas later we had told each other all the stories we had about home, former girlfriends, and past athletic achievements. Very carefully, I drove us back to the base.

I awoke late the next morning with little memory of that drive home. My headache was reminding me that I had consumed way too many Margaritas when Geary came by with the news that we were being deployed back to Vietnam. Fast track promotions had come through and we had another celebration ahead. Collins was promoted from Petty Officer 1st Class to Chief Petty Officer. Rivera was promoted to Petty Officer 1st Class, Castanaro made Chief Petty Officer, White was promoted to Gunnery Sergeant.

Gunnery Sergeant (GySgt), a unique rank in the United States Marine Corps, is a specialized non-commissioned officer who manages firepower and logistics for a company-sized unit of Marines. Promotion to Gunnery Sergeant requires a great deal of leadership skill and an excellent command of specialized knowledge of weapons systems and combat logistics. A Gunnery Sergeant is usually known informally by the nickname "Gunny".

We now had a Gunnery Sergeant, White, and three Chief Petty Officers, Guadanoli, Castanaro and Collins, on the team.

We had two weeks to get in-shape physically and mentally to go back in-country. We were running 5 miles each morning before breakfast. After breakfast, the platoon had language training and then target practice at Pendleton before lunch. Afternoons included tactical training, jungle survival studies, and weight training. Evenings I watched the news with some amazement. It was clear that the reporters attempted to show the war in a politically correct way. I heard on the news that only the poor were drafted to serve as cannon fodder in a war that we had no business being involved in as a country. Everyone in my platoon was a volunteer and we were going back in-country, ostensibly, to preserve freedom for the South Vietnamese that our country had agreed to protect.

CHAPTER 15

Back to the War

May 1966

Tan Son Nhut airport was busier now than last time around, but just as hot and sticky. We were back just in time for the rainy season. Instead of a long bus ride this time, there was a Chinook helicopter waiting to ferry us to our base. It was loaded with supplies headed to My Tho and we squeezed in. My team was still intact for our second tour. Exiting the Chinook into the 90 degree 90 per cent relative humidity of the Mekong Delta with all the familiar smells was to quote Yogi Berra, "De ja vu all over again."

The new CO was Cmdr. Albert Costello, USN who was in charge of riverine activities and the SEALs in the Delta. We reported in and received our hootch assignments. We were to stand down and get settled. The living quarters were a pleasant surprise. We had wooden floors made from the pallets that supplies had come in on. We had walls and two windows. The biggest surprise was a window mounted air conditioner. Wow! This was living.

Collins showed up with a case, 4 six packs, of Budweiser. A welcome present from the team that we replaced and was heading home after their 180 days in country. All in all, this was better than I had expected. We had operated in this area previously and knew the terrain much better than our brief foray up north in Central Highlands last January. We were the Green Faces and we owned the swamp.

Geary yelled from outside the door, "Lt you have a visitor."

"Hey Indian'" Tommy greeted me as he burst through the door.

"Hey Marine", I responded.

Herndon, Thomas C., 1st Lt USMC was a sight for sore eyes. Tommy had joined the 3rd Force Recon and was working with the1st Battalion 5th Marines in the Rung Sat Special Zone as a platoon Leader. He had qualified for Force Recon at Camp Lejeune, North Carolina.

Marine Force Reconnaissance companies are special operations capable forces that perform deep reconnaissance and direct action support. They are responsible for operating independently behind enemy lines performing unconventional special operations. They provided special ops support in the Rung Sat Special Zone for Marine amphibious operations. The 26th Marine Expeditionary that included Tommy's 3rd FORCON was shorthanded and had combined elements of the 2nd Force Recon.

Rigorous training had trimmed Tommy's bulk down to bone and gristle. His youthful aggressiveness that had made him an all-star on the football field had given way to the patience of a predator. Tommy was one of the predators feared by the VC in the vile swamp of the Mekong Delta.

After I introduced Tommy to the team, we had about an hour to catch up before he had to go. We talked about old times in Texas, his sister's marriage, and that I had just missed seeing his parents last month. We said our goodbyes. His platoon was headed down river to search out a gook encampment thought to be interdicting shipping on the Mekong River near the Bassac River confluence.

I made arrangements for my platoon to be ferried across the river to the firing range. We would spend the afternoon zeroing our weapons after transporting them with us from Coronado. I had a Colt AR-16 5.56 mm assault rifle accurized by the USMC armorers, a Colt Model 1911-A1 .45 caliber sidearm, and my trusty Ithaca Model 37 12-gauge shotgun. Guadanoli had his M60 machine gun that fired the NATO 7.62x51mm from a disintegrating belt of M13 links. It weighed about 23 pounds and fire up to 650 rounds per minute with a maximum effective range of 1200 yards. It was a moose to carry in difficult terrain, but it saved our butts time and time again. He also carried a Model 1911A1 semi-automatic pistol. SEALs were allowed some flexibility in their choice of personal weapons and we had a variety including the accurized M14 that Collins carried. The M14 also fired the 7.62x51mm (.308 Winchester) round that was heavier than the M16's 5.56x45mm (.223 Remington) cartridge carried by most. The Marine Corps armorers had replaced the wooden stock on Collins' M14 with a fiberglass stock that would not swell in the heat and moisture. The M14 had extended range and 2,470 ft-lbs of muzzle energy that could penetrate heavy cover. In addition, we all carried M61 fragmentation grenades. The M61 was a M26A1 grenade with a jungle clip attached to the safety lever. This was to prevent the safety lever from flying off and allowing detonation if the pin gets pulled off accidentally by jungle vegetation.

After a two-hour sighting in session to make absolutely sure that each of our weapons was zeroed in and would go bang when we pulled the trigger, we caught a ride back across the river to our base. The shadows were growing longer as I left the mess hall. We were back in-country and I expected that we would receive orders to go back to work tomorrow. Orders came quickly, as I expected. I was intercepted on my walk back to the hootch by a young Marine Private with word from our CO, Cmdr. Costello, to come forthwith.

The Navy does not salute uncovered (without a hat or cover on your head). I removed my boonie hat as I entered and said, "Lt Stryker, reporting as ordered, sir."

"Sit", he said motioning to a folding chair next to his desk. "We have strong suspicions that the VC have encamped by the Bassac and Mekong Rivers. The Marines were ambushed there this morning by an estimated platoon-sized force. The Marine's Force Recon platoon suffered heavy losses then pushed the VC back. They were transported back to My Tho and reported in about an hour ago. We want to get eyes on the ground to find their base of operations and to supply coordinates for an air attack. Select members of your team to be inserted by PBR tomorrow."

I hurried back to the team to let them know about tomorrow's mission. I said that I wanted two volunteers to accompany me and Guadanoli and Collins immediately volunteered.

I knew that it was Tommy's platoon that got hit, so I went over to the Marine's HQ to check on Tommy. SSgt. Fisher from Tommy's platoon was there and he knew that Tommy and I were close. He drew long on his cigarette and then proceeded to tell me that Tommy was gone. They had walked into an ambush and the VC had mined the trail. They had three KIA's and eight peanuts or wounded. They picked up some pieces. Fisher said that he was sure they were pieces of Lt. Herndon. Tommy had tripped a booby trapped claymore type mine that blasted shrapnel and tore him apart.

I went back to my hootch to compose a letter to Tommy's parents. Writing this letter forced me to remember and evaluate things that I had suppressed during both tours of duty. Tommy's ex Gwen had broken his heart, affected his NFL career, and now was part of the misinformed Hollywood crowd spreading dis-information about the war. This suddenly became very personal.

Along with the Marines, we patrolled the swamp from the South China Sea and the confluence of the Bassac and Mekong Rivers to the Kien Phong Province that bordered Cambodia. Some 150 kilometers that included swamp, jungle and rice fields on highlands that extended west to Cambodia. The rigorous SEAL training and the perseverance of our men under atrocious conditions had been slowly wresting control of the Rung Sat from the VC. They called us the "green faces" and placed rewards on our heads.

There were patches of sometimes dry ground here and there with connecting trails that were often submerged in the crawling slime of the swamp. The difficult area served Charlie well as strategic encampments and caches for rice and ordnance. We felt that we owned the Rung Sat and Charlie was a trespasser.

But it wasn't fair. Combat taught us that quickly. The best and the brightest, the most patriotic, even the heroic were torn apart both physically and mentally. Our peers went to grad school and got on prime time yelling communist slogans to gullible news reporters. Hollywood idols grandstanded with the VC. We just did our duty. We sweated and cursed and bled and died for what we believed in - God, Honor, Country.

To the media, we were all pot smoking baby killers.

It wasn't fair. Tommy had almost completed his tour of duty. He was okay this morning. Tommy was physically intimidating, very efficient under extreme conditions, a trained predator who had survived and prevailed until today. Tomorrow at 0900, he would have been airlifted out of our base in My Tho about some 70 klicks south-southwest of Saigon and rotated to stateside training duty at Camp Pendleton north of San Diego. He had orders for an early out to meet the Marine Corps training needs.

Incoming hit the base at 2135 hours. Somewhere on base, they were preparing to send parts of Tommy, maybe it was him, it was hard to tell, home for burial with full military honors.

I had to write a letter to two loving parents whose all-American son would never have the opportunity of a full life. He went before his season as my native American forbearers would have lamented. The visions of parading students, draft dodgers, and misguided publicity seeking celebrities made concentrating on the words difficult. Why the best…it wasn't his time. The deep-seated virus of hatred made the task of writing this awful letter even more unsavory. I killed VC, but I hadn't hated them. The injustice of seeing our country's best shredded and bagged while the losers, quitters, and vocal cowards were glorified by our people back home absolutely tormented me, but I did my job. Tommy was my best and only real close friend. My spirit brother. Man, I got to change jobs.

CHAPTER 16

Revenge

May 1966

The other men in my platoon depended on me to do my job and I knew that I could depend on them. And, I had orders for our next mission. Guadanoli and Collins were waiting for me at 0530 hours. We loaded onto the PBR captained by Campbell, Thomas R., PO-1 USN and his crew of three sailors. They would insert us down river and stand by to extract us on 30 minutes notice.

Both Guadanoli and Collins knew that I was looking to count coup for my spirit brother. We had discussed our approach and that we would avoid the trails and their booby traps. Best guess was that the gook encampment was less than a two klicks from the main river on a dry island in the swamp. We had a handwritten map captured from the VC that indicated the location and it looked like a canal connected it to the main river. Our plan was to wade with the snakes and leeches to confirm the VC presence, call in the coordinates, and get out before the Air Force or Marine pilots blew it away. My revenge would be delivered from the sky.

It was very slow, arduous going. We climbed over mangrove roots and stopped every 30 minutes for de-leeching. We were operating on adrenaline and every sense was on high alert as we closed to about 200 meters from our objective.

I signaled to Guadanoli and Collins to stay back and cover me as a crept ahead. My father's training in stealth and woodcraft in order to get close to wild game in the hills paid dividends as I slowly and as quietly as I could closed the gap. I covered about 35 meters in the next 20 minutes to gain a clear view through the foliage. The VC were right where we expected them to be located. It was a dry Nipa Palm covered island with a tributary stream or canal flowing on the south side.

I could smell their camp and see their hootches. I perceived more than saw a slight movement just 20 meters to my left. A gook sentry was posted there and he was alert, scanning the edge of the foliage.

As I sat quietly on a mangrove root with my legs in the knee deep water, I watched the camp and confirmed that it contained about 40 VC. I saw no heavy ordnance. This was an isolated camp and supply depot that was provisioned by sampans coming up from the river. Finally, the sentry stood and walked toward the nearest hootch and called for his replacement to come and relieve him.

Quietly, I retreated back to Guadanoli and Collins. We retraced the way that we came in for some 200 meters before calling in the coordinates.

The coordinates were confirmed and relayed to the Air Force. I then called for our extraction.

Past experience was that the jungle would began to erupt indiscriminately and we needed to be elsewhere as fast as possible. It took us a full 30 minutes going as fast as we could through the swamp to get to our extraction point. As we swam out to the PBR, fast moving shadows passed overhead. The jungle position that we had just vacated erupted as I heard the jets scream in a power climb. There had been a last minute change, probably based on aircraft availability. The three Marine Corps F-4 Phantoms hedge hopped in and obliterated the camp on the first run. The second run was just for confirmation that the camp was destroyed.

God, I love the Marine Corps pilots. Instead of dropping their payload from up high where wind and other factors could cause their bombs to stray, the USMC pilots were at tree top level. They didn't miss. The shadows of the F-4 Phantoms flashed overhead. The jungle erupted and then we heard them in their power climb.

As soon as we were aboard, Campbell hit the throttles. He spun the PBR in its own length. The twin jet drives driven by Detroit Diesels pushed us up on plane and sped us away. The three of us stripped off our clothes and pulled off leeches on the trip back.

Completing my after action report, I requested two days of liberty for Guadanoli, Collins, and me. The CO granted my request. I planned on hitching a ride to Saigon and getting drunk. Joe and Mitch would be on their own.

The scene in Saigon was both hectic and depressing. The streets were clogged with traffic of all kinds. Trucks, bicycles, motor bikes, and foot traffic was everywhere. After weeks in the bush it smelled very different and the ambient noise accosted my ears. The Vietnamese like beer and the local Tiger beer was decent. After two beers, the Vietnamese bar girls began to look more attractive as I fended off their broken English advances. They were motivated to get their hands on American dollars. I knew how many cases of venereal disease had been treated at the base and I, personally, didn't find them all that enticing. I'm no prude, but I am supposed to be an officer and a gentleman.

I decided that I wasn't going to get drunk, so I went to the Continental Hotel and got a room assigned. The Continental was a relic of French Colonial days. It had a flower-filled courtyard with wandering peacocks and you could smell the freshly baked bread from the kitchen. A long, hot shower and uninterrupted sleep was the order of the day.

At 0400 hours, I was wide awake. I went downstairs and found the open sided terrace known as the Continental Shelf. There were some guests enjoying coffee in the pre-dawn hours. I ordered a cup of excellent coffee. Several tables away, I recognized Major Cashin. He was the Marine in charge during the Phoenix Program that we worked with on my last tour of duty. He was deep in discussion with the CIA guy, DaSilva, that I also remembered from that mission. I had mixed emotions about both them They did their job and obtained relevant intelligence including some that my platoon used on our missions. The brutal torture methods that they used to successfully obtain that information was chilling. I decided that I would head over to the airport and hitch a ride back to My Tho. Arriving at Tan Son Nhut airbase in time for breakfast, I was surprised at the mess tent. Both Guadanoli and Collins were back and having breakfast. We were all on the same train of thought and anxious to get back to the platoon. Guadanoli finished his second cup of coffee and volunteered to find us transportation back to My Tho. The platoon was our family and we felt the need to be there.

CHAPTER 17

The Rabbit Hole

June 1966

The Air Force had a begun massive defoliation campaign called Operation Ranch Hand to deny the enemy forces cover. They heavily sprayed the Demilitarized Zone, along the South Vietnamese borders with Cambodia and Laos, and the mangrove forests in the Rung Sat Special Zone along the river approaches to Saigon and in the Mekong Delta's Ca Mau Peninsula. Agent Orange was the code name for one of the worst herbicides and it got its name from the orange striped 55 gallon drums that it was shipped to Vietnam in from the Monsanto and Dow Chemical corporations.

Some areas had been extensively napalmed. Burned leaving nothing but rocks, dirt, and crispy critters of all kinds including human.

We had been airlifted to Can Tho some 50 kilometers southwest of My Tho and then boarded a PBR on the Hua River. We were headed upriver to a small village that we called the Rabbit Hole just south of Long Xuyen. The VC had been hitting the city nightly with mortars and then disappearing in the Rabbit Hole. It had been bombed, sprayed, and napalmed. Our job was to find out where they went during the day.

My SEAL Platoon was comprised of two squads that called for six men each, but like most units in country we were shorthanded and were just five men on each squad. I counted myself and served double duty as a squad leader. My squad was needed on this reconnaissance mission. Geary, White, Jones, and Guadanoli joined me. Collins was sick with a stomach flu and Guadanoli, the other squad leader, took his place. We carried extra ammo, grenades and three days of MRE's. Our transport was a PBR captained by Campbell PO-1. Campbell had successfully transported us on previous missions and I knew his boat crew. His Gunners Mate, Posey, was a real wise-ass joker, but I think he had heard stories about the "Green Faces". White, who was very black and looked like an NFL linebacker, gave Posey a vicious scowl when he came on board. Posey stayed clear of us. We went upriver saying very little and mentally rehearsing our mission.

We inserted at the Rabbit Hole. It was defoliated and burned. Geary took the point and we carefully picked our way through the ash going single file to minimize the potential of mines and booby traps. After almost two hours with no sounds and nothing moving, no birds, snakes, or critters of any kind, I signaled a smoke break.

The low ridge north of us had some surviving trees and brush. It was another long hike. We would make our way to that ridge and then dig in for the night. If Charlie came down to the river's edge tonight, we would have him. Jones whistled for my attention and signaled to come. He had found a tunnel entrance. There were fresh signs that both exited and entered the tunnel entrance. We had heard stories about the extensive tunnel network in the highlands around Chou Lai. The water table was so high around the Mekong Delta that we had not seen any significant tunneling by the VC. Here we were on slightly higher ground and the Rabbit Hole was aptly named.

I surmised that the gooks spent their time during the day underground and came out at night to harass the villages. It wasn't our job nor was it within our realistic capabilities for the five of us to crawl into the tunnel network. I called in the coordinates and my action plan.

We had enough C4 explosive with us to close up this tunnel entrance. We would explore the surrounding area for other entrances and then head up the ridge for the night's reconnaissance. Guadanoli set the C4 and after it blew we inspected the tunnel entrance or where it had been. We found another tunnel about 35 meters away partially hidden by some weeds. Guadanoli again set the explosive charges and blew it up.

We didn't find any other tunnels. Hopefully, we had trapped any VC inside like rats in a cage. We made our way up to the low ridge north of the defoliated area and found a small clearing where we could activity all the way to the river.

At 2300 hours Jones woke me for my turn at surveillance. It had been all quiet. Fortunately, this was one of the few clear nights without rain. Jones had thankfully heated up some coffee for me. I poured a cup and took up my position.

The gooks must have been on my schedule. I barely got through a cup of coffee when I saw there was movement only 50 meters downhill. Another hidey hole that we had missed. A squad of gooks filed down toward the river. I watched until I knew their approximate destination on the river bank. I crawled back and woke up the other four guys. Calling in the info on the gook squad, we took positions that would adequately turn the tunnel where they exited into a kill zone if anymore gooks ventured out.

The bright flash of bursting 500 pound bombs followed by the sound of multiple explosions and the trembling ground that we sat on signaled the Air Force had arrived. It was over in four minutes. We maintained our positions to catch any retreating survivors in our kill zone.

The rest of the night passed uneventfully. At day break, we had coffee and MRE eggs, then saddled up. Carefully, we worked our way down to the river to evaluate and report damage from last night's attack. Geary found the first dead gook. After a thorough search, we found the remains of nine VC and two 60mm mortars. These were US Army issued M224 mortars that had been captured by the VC. They were far more efficient than most of the handmade VC mortars. The M224 had a maximum range of 2.17 miles, could fire 30 rounds per minute, and only weighed 40 pounds.

The VC had a very limited industrial base and used basically a homemade portable mortar called the Sky Horse. The weapon was formed by using two-inch metal pipe and a folding bipod support base that was bolted and wired together. The result was a crude but serviceable light weight artillery piece that could fire 50.8mm rounds at about 10 rounds per minute manually muzzle loaded.

Calling in our report, I was told to take a defensive position and hold until further notice. There was a significant action in progress and no assets were immediately available to extract us. By 1700 hours I was getting concerned that we might overnight in position. It was reasonable to assume that the VC would be reconnoitering the area soon.

Geary was carrying our communications gear and serving as my RM on this mission. We were sharing a bomb crater by the river's edge and swapping stories of home. Joe Geary was from Waltham, Massachusetts just outside of Boston. As a Navy Chief Petty Officer with eleven years' experience, he was a steady hand. After being in the surface Navy for seven years, he had volunteered for the SEALs. He had two kids and an ex-wife who had filed for divorce during his seventh year in the Navy. Extended sea duty had made for a difficult home life.

AK-47's have a unique sound. Bullets buzzed by and some dirt got kicked up stinging my face. The chatter of AK's was coming from east of our position.

The AK was the primary infantry weapon of the Vietcong and North Vietnamese Army (NVA). People's Republic of China was the primary supplier of these assault rifles based on the original Russian design by Mikhail Kalashnikov. It was sturdy, reliable, and relatively light weight. It fired a 7.62x39mm projectile. The tumbling action of the bullet at impact created a large entry wound and severe tissue damage. Coupled with its rapid fire capability this meant accuracy was a bit less important and reduced training time. The AK-47 had a 30 round capacity and for overall combat reliability and durability was judged by many to be superior to the U.S. manufactured AR-16.

The gooks were east us on the river bank less than 100 meters away. The defoliation left no cover between us. We had a small advantage. We were dug in, slightly up hill, and were very accurate marksmen. Plus, we had Guadanoli with his M60. I called for air support and supplied our position. Support was on the way and we needed to hold our position until they arrived. I figured that there were fifteen VC attacking us. We were outnumbered three to one.

I switched my M16 to semi-automatic fire for long range accuracy. Guadanoli kept up fire with his M60. The rest of us would pick our targets as the gooks popped up to return fire. It was like a fatal game of whack-a-mole. We had them pinned down but we were not going anywhere either.

Within ten long minutes the fire fight was over when two Bell Iroquois "Hueys" showed up. The Cobra gunships with their mounted M60's began raking the enemy positions like two ballet dancers acting together. It was beautiful to watch. The Navy sometimes referred to the gunships as Sharks and the troop carrying Slicks or unarmed Hueys as Dolphins. Our ride home came in behind the Sharks to a quiet LZ.

I sat in the doorway of the Dolphin with my feet on the skid as the adrenaline leeched out of me on the ride home. I watched the ground whiz by beneath me as I decompressed.

Man, I got to change jobs.

CHAPTER 18

Thanh Phu

July 1966

My team was being airlifted with extra supplies by Chinook to the district capitol city of Thanh Phu in the extreme southern section of the Rung Sat Special Zone in Ben Tre Province. Operation Game Warden had been initiated and it was the SEALs responsibility to stalk the Vietcong in the Rung Sat Special Zone.

Ben Tre Province was rural with a population of 100,000 spread over 401 square kilometers or about 155 square miles. The Ham Luong River is to the north, south is the Chien River, and east is the South China Sea. Highway 57 runs from Thanh Phu in the Ben Tre Province to Vinh Long in the center of the Mekong Delta and connects to National Highway 1A which is the main thoroughfare to Saigon 135 kilometers (84 miles) away. Control of Thanh Phu and the surrounding area was strategically important.

The VC had been visiting the surrounding villages for food and recruiting the young and fit men, women, and even children. Village chiefs that resisted were beaten and some were executed for an example. The 1st Battalion 5th Marines had been active in the area and their search and destroy missions had located many gook supply caches and camps back in the swamp. The VC responded by increasing their level of conscripting more villagers. They needed to be routed out of the swamp and banished.

That was our job.

South Vietnam is about 8 degrees north of the equator and has a humid tropical climate with an average 55 inches of rainfall mostly in the rainy season from May to November. The Rung Sat was rural with a myriad of crisscrossing streams, mangrove swamps and higher fertile ground that was heavily covered with forest or head high brush if not cultivated.

The Marine Force Recon unit was very shorthanded after several months of being in the Rung Sat and under almost daily conflict. They were being re-deployed up north to Da Nang and expecting replacements. The Marines had dropped 3rd FORCON to non-combat ready status.

Capt. Lovejoy, 3rd FORCON company commander, welcomed me and the team. Capt. James D. Lovejoy was a short, powerful looking fire plug of a Marine. Probably 5 feet 8 inches and 200 pounds. I asked the Capt. to familiarize my platoon with the area and he gave us a detailed briefing on the geography and what to expect. His company's 2nd platoon had a significant fire fight with and company sized VC force just two days ago. They suffered two KIA and five wounded. Outnumbered about four to one they held their own and got lifted out. The Capt. thought the main camp was in the Mo Cay District, but there were small encampments and supply caches in several other areas that he indicated for us.

The remaining 3rd FORCON Marines were airlifted out on the next morning to join replacements in Da Nang. This was now our show. Our SEAL platoon's mobile support team (MST) was on the way navigating the river system and they were expected by dark.

The MSTs were small groups of men specially trained to support SEAL operations. MSTs operated a variety of boats that included the light, medium, and heavy SEAL support craft.

As the shadows got long, Petty Officer Campbell now our MST Chief motored in with his 31 foot PBR loaded with more supplies and ammo. He was towing a STAB (SEAL Team Assault Boat). STAB's were modified Boston Whalers about 20 feet long with twin outboard motors that could push them at 35 knots. They could carry a SEAL squad and had a two-man crew. Armament was four 7.62mm machine guns, 40mm Mk 18 grenade launcher. The fiberglass hull was not armor plated and small arms fire could literally transverse both gunwales.

Much to our chagrin Posey was still his Gunners Mate on the PBR. SSgt. White was already grumbling something about kicking his white ass. Rick White wasn't making a racist comment, there was no one more good natured and dependable in a tight spot. He just didn't like Posey's wise ass attitude and nonstop motor mouth.

It was my idea to put White as the first in line to grab off loaded supplies from Posey. They had to work together, might as well start now.

Campbell would provide and/or dispatch either the PBR or the STAB for insertion and extraction as well as logistical support. Air support was at Tan Song Nhut and not always available.

We spent the evening getting the former FORCON camp rearranged to suit our needs and getting supplies stowed. The Marines were leaving a short platoon of 38 men under 2nd Lt. Waller for camp support and protection. Capt. Lovejoy had walked the perimeter defense with me when we checked in and I decided to walk it again with Guadanoli before dark. Unlike the Army or Marine base camps that we had been assigned to previously with several hundred men, we were 16 guys, my 10-man platoon plus the MST crew, and 2nd Lt Waller's platoon. Fortunately, we were on a peninsular that jutted out into the river and had water on three sides. Guadanoli and I discussed the probability that the gooks knew that we had just arrived and that our defensive positions may be weak because we were new. We agreed that we should alternate squads with one squad staying in camp when possible. I planned on taking the fight to the enemy.

The "Green Faces" were here. They called us that because of the green camouflage paint that we used to stop the shine from our faces. We would disrupt the VC supply and troop movements by using guerrilla and anti-guerrilla tactics. We would bring a personal war to the gooks in their previously safe area.

I assumed that we were surrounded by Vietcong sympathizers. The villagers that initially did not support them were terrorized until they became supportive. The Army and Marines could try to win their hearts. We were here to destroy the enemy and would also conduct a psychological war to create an unspoken balance of terror. We would gain a reputation as fearsome and extraordinary warriors so that Charlie would not want to go against us.

Campbell's crew would stand watch and be part of our 24-hour rotation. The river sailors weren't happy about that, but they all understood that there wasn't anyone else to cover that duty. The thought crossed my mind that the gooks would know that most of the Marines had left. I wondered if they would test us tonight and I wanted us to be ready.

We were a lucky team and our luck held out. It was an uneventful night.

After breakfast, I called Campbell over and we discussed the Plan of the Day. His STAB, a 20 foot weaponized Boston Whaler, would insert Castanaro's five-man squad about a klick down river to reconnoiter east. The squad would then turn back north about a klick and then turn west back to the river opposite our camp. We needed to clear the immediate area on the opposite side of the river and assurance that no gooks would lob mortars at us from across the water. This entire area is crisscrossed with small rivers and canals. It is heavily forested with some savannahs of dense brush and grass that were 6-8 feet tall. The fertile soil grows rice and fruit where cleared and cultivated. The mangrove swamps downriver and close to the South China Sea are nearly impenetrable.

Castanaro's squad boarded the STAB and departed at 0830 hours. I had spoken briefly with Rivera, his RM carrying the squad's communications gear, to stay asshole to belly button with his squad leader. I needed regular updates during the mission. We were their only potential help if they ran into trouble. Gun ships from Tan Son Nhut, if available, were 25 minutes out.

The rest of us would spend the day improving our defenses by filling and placing as many sand bags as we could in strategic locations.

Castanaro called in at 1145 hours. They found a burned out village where there had been six hootches and about 10 acres that had been cleared and cultivated for some type of fruit trees and another 10 acres of rice. The fields had been abandoned for awhile and the jungle was reclaiming the land.

The squad moved on turning north and forded several small creeks. Castanaro called back in at 1330. They came across a trail leading back towards the river and our camp that was booby trapped with small mines (called Dap loi or step-on mines) on the trail and on each side to catch others coming to assist. These small mines were designed to cripple the feet and legs They were simply made from empty .50 caliber shell casings filled with gun powder and scrap metal. The casing is sealed with wax and placed in a bamboo cylinder with a small nail in the bottom. It's buried in the ground so only the wax on top is showing. When stepped on the casing is pressed into the nail which then blows scrap metal in the lower extremities. It is rarely fatal, but causes very bloody and painful damage.

Castanaro suggested that we set some of our own booby traps to catch any gook patrols coming by to engage us. Good idea. It would be our early warning system on the eastside.

Campbell personally captained the Assault Boat to extract the squad and returned the squad to our camp 1730 hours. The evening rain was just starting as Castanaro gave his after action report that we relayed to Cmdr. Zanke. I gave my situation analysis and that we would be checking out a village northwest of our position. It appeared to be a group of about a dozen hootches with a stream just east with a road that ran northward parallel to the river. Cultivated rice fields stretched to the west. I wanted the team to have firsthand knowledge of our surrounding territory. Just as important, I wanted the surrounding villagers to know that we were here and to be feared.

I believe that respect and fear are closely related and among the strongest emotions that we humans universally harbor. My "Green Faces" would make a strong and immediate impression. The VC would soon learn to fear us.

After a quick breakfast briefing, we saddled up carrying just our web gear with some snacks, extra water, and ammo. We spread out and carefully walked the roadside looking for mines and booby traps. Rules of engagement were to shoot anyone carrying a weapon and destroy all caches of ordnance found.

There was zero traffic on the road. As we approached the village it was eerily quiet. We spread out and slowly worked our way forward. I motioned to Jones to move over to the right side of the village. Mama sans and little kids came out to see us as we entered. We were looking at hostile faces.

A pajama clad figure dashed out of the second hootch on the left headed for the bush. I shot him at 15 meters. I had my Ithaca 12-gauge with buckshot and at that range it is very lethal.

The wailing and yelling immediately started as a mama san ran over to him as the life blood left his body. Geary on the left and White on the right began searching the hootches. White brought out a young gook from the hootch on the right. The second hootch on the left yielded an AK-47 and 3 extra 30 round clips of ammo.

This was a VC village next door to us. It was obvious from their body language and hostile looks that they hated us. We found two more AK's and I ordered the hootches where we found the weapons burned. We took the captured gook and the weapons with us. We had no translator with us, but I thought that HQ might want to interrogate him. Our prisoner resolved that when he bolted for the jungle even with his hands secured behind his back. White 3-tapped his M16 and the gook was history.

We were not prepared to take prisoners. Any gook carrying a weapon or doing any threatening act was quickly dispatched. We knew that the VC in this area executed and sometimes mutilated any wounded U.S. military personnel that they found. This episode would be related to our enemies – beware the "Green Faces" are here.

We would have a squad interdicting VC activities in this area daily and, as we learned the turf, we would terrorized the VC at night. We had trained with the CIA to conduct psychological warfare. It was an effective way to use terror to neutralize the villagers' sympathy for the Viet Cong. It became a question of who they feared the most. I decided, with the discrete agreement of my boss, that we would become the most fearsome warriors in the swamp. Charlie would fear "Green Faces".

In order to effectively achieve that goal and be successful, as Platoon-Officer-Charge, I also had to do my best to get my men home safely and in one piece. Like virtually everyone in combat, our hope was to return home to our loved ones in one piece. Our motivation amid the chaos, noise, and abject terror of combat was to do our job and protect our brothers.

July 21, 1966, the immediate area around our camp was mostly secure. We had cleared the area of brush and sniper hides. We had two rows of razor wire around the perimeter and mines in between. We had improved and fortified the sandbags around our hootches. Tonight, Guadanoli's squad was headed back in the bush to raid and terrorize a known VC village about 5 klicks up river.

I was headed down river with Alpha Squad for another night-time raid. We heard from a friendly village chief that the VC camped there had been pressuring his village for recruits and food. The 20-foot STAB (SEAL Team Assault Boat) was captained by Gunner's Mate Posey and he overshot our insertion point. It was dark when we saw the evening fires of the VC village on the shore. We were still skimming along throwing up a wake and the twin outboards were roaring.

I got that oh shit feeling. We couldn't slow down faster enough and I knew that we were about to be detected. Without the element of surprise, we were seconds away from being toast. As the 20 foot Boston Whaler slowed down, Collins got on the 7.62mm machine gun mounted on the bow and Geary manned the 40mm grenade launcher. We could see the gooks illuminated by the fires running to get their weapons. Posey turned the STAB into the current to give us a stabile shooting platform and the illuminated village was a target rich kill zone.

The evening erupted in gunfire and grenade explosions. The VC were cut down as they emerged from their hootches with weapons. We counted coup and my Shoshone ancestors would be proud. Less than two minutes into the shore bombardment, I signaled Posey to get us out fast. We had turned an oversight into a success. We sped away at full throttle and I thanked whatever gods maybe for our continued good luck.

Campbell's PBR docked the next morning bringing Guadanoli's squad back from their night time raid upriver. The squad had inserted undetected and worked their way to the VC village. His Bravo Squad had the village under surveillance before dark and had seen armed VC there. They had hit the small village hard at 0230 hours and skedaddled out for extraction with no casualties. Guadanoli estimated that they killed 5 VC. The Green Faces had struck again.

CHAPTER 19

Marine Support

August 1966

In a few short weeks, we had become the dominant force around Thanh Phu. We increased our kill count weekly and continued to be very lucky. A couple of minor injuries, but nothing serious. We were primary targets for the VC snipers. The Marine sentry on duty last night had been shot at while on the western perimeter. White and Castanaro volunteered to a stealthy patrol outside our perimeter to track the sniper.

White and Castanaro were back an hour after daylight with two ears. The sniper and his spotter would bother us no more.

Operation Game Warden was initiated in the Rung Sat Special Zone. Task Force 116 now had the responsibility to deny the National Liberation Front and its military arm the Viet Cong access to resources in the Mekong Delta. It included Naval Forces, Marine Artillery and air support to launch rapid surprise attacks on the many small VC ports scattered throughout the delta.

The Marines had established control in the northern part of Ben Tre Province where the higher ground supported rice and fruit farming. A marine platoon led by Lt. Devers was dispatched to our camp. This bolstered our camp defense and allowed us to have both our squads out at the same time to increase our effectiveness. Our psychological warfare techniques were beginning to pay dividends. Some village chieftains feared and respected us more than the VC and came to us with intelligence.

The Central Intelligence Agency had a history of using the SEALs in covert operations. They sponsored operations to target the execution or capture of North Vietnamese Army personnel and Vietcong sympathizers. This just increased the psychological benefit of our activities.

We were encouraged to capture VC leadership for interrogation. Yes, the CIA's torture techniques were virtually always successful.

Guadanoli's squad came back after a two days of reconnaissance southwest along a navigable tributary to the Chien River. They had found a major VC encampment. There were four sizable wooden boats and several sampans pulled up on the river bank. A unformed NVA (North Vietnamese Army) officer was sighted there. Guadanoli's report generated lots of interest in the NVA officer.

Our CO, Cmdr. Zanke, got back to us that the NVA officer was wanted for interrogation, if we could bring him in. There was speculation that he was General Ngo Than Nyugen and had responsibility for the North's logistical support of the Viet Cong operating in the southern area. We would be outnumbered and that goes against military training to attack with overwhelming force. There was no indication that General Nyugen would be there tomorrow and we were the nearest and best choice to get out there now.

Cmdr. Zanke got air support reserved for an operation tonight. Guadanoli's squad would catch four hours rest and then the whole platoon would saddle up to be in position for the air attack. We would shut the back door and then mop up and hopefully capture the General. Petty Officer Campbell would come up river with his Patrol Boat's twin 12.7 mm (.50 caliber) Browning heavy machine guns in the bow, an aft M-60 (7.62 mm) machine gun, and Mark 19 40 mm grenade launcher to block any river escape attempt. Campbell would continue to cover the river during our mop up and then extract us.

With Guadanoli's squad to lead us back to the VC encampment, we saddled up for a five hour walk through the brush. Thankfully, the rain held off. We were able to move more quickly than anticipated because of Guadanoli's local knowledge of the trails. Reaching our position blocking the VC back door 30 minutes in advance of schedule, gave us time to quietly dig in defensive positions.

The Air Force arrived on time. The AC-47 Spooky or Puff the Magic Dragon opened up with its Gatling guns. Puff circled slowly in a left hand turn as the three 7.62mm General Electric mini guns that could fire 100 rounds per second raked the VC camp. The devastating fire was ripping the camp apart. We heard Campbell's PBR coming upstream. The PBR's grenade launcher added to noise and exploded shrapnel in the camp. Gunners Mate, Posey, did his job with the forward twin machine guns ripping up the hulls of the beached wooden boats and sampans.

The surviving gooks had only one way out and we were there. We opened up as they entered our kill zone. The firefight was over in less than 15 minutes.

Collins nudged me and pointed. A VC about 15 meters away was crouched over and limping away. In one swift movement, I swiveled and shot. It was like jump shooting ruffed grouse in my native mountains. We spent the next hour mopping up, destroying ordnance, and checking the smoldering ruins and bodies for any intelligence. There were no survivors. The NVA general was dead, but we found papers and handwritten maps that we would bring out with us.

He had meticulous handwritten records and maps of the local area down to the trails and which tributaries were navigable. The Marines had a Chieu Hoi, Vietnamese interpreter and interrogator, who said this was good stuff and sent it up the chain of command, but not before I could review them. His maps were much better than ours and indicated which tributary streams we could navigate for insertion and extraction. I went over these carefully with now Chief Campbell, our MST (Riverine Mobile Support Team) leader. We could use this to our advantage. Campbell would know in advance if a PBR or STAB could make up the river.

Campbell was assigned to River Division 53 My Tho and had orders to bring his PBR in for maintenance to a support ship on the Ham Luong River north of us. He would be gone 3 days and that would leave us with only a STAB, the 20-foot assault craft capable of transporting a SEAL squad plus two crewmen.

The captured river maps showed a small tributary to the My Tho river that to me was a strategic location to control a series of small rural villages that were upstream. The villagers most likely would transport their produce and goods downstream to the My Tho River to trade. I suspected that the Vietcong would control that flow of goods by having a camp somewhere at or between the first village and the confluence with the My Tho River.

Rather than wait for Campbell's return, I planned for us to ferry a squad from Golf Platoon on the STAB to an insertion point just upriver from the confluence. The 20 foot Boston Whaler had twin outboards that were fairly noisy. We would insert far from the expected location of the VC camp and approach on foot. Sneaking and peeking. We inserted just as the moon was rising. According to the captured map, there was a dirt track that could support bicycle and foot traffic along the river. We followed the trail for about a kilometer when I could smell smoke. We took to the brush for cover and slowly went another 35 meters.

Just as suspected the VC had a camp right at a bend in the river where the current would drift most traffic into close quarters. We studied the camp and could not discern any sentries. I wanted to wait until the camp was sound asleep before unleashing devastation.

I spread the 5-man squad around the 3 sides of the camp away from the river making absolutely sure that each man would know the location of every squad member. We had about 20 meters between each man with an open kill zone. White was positioned with his M60 on the downriver side. Castanaro, Geary, and Collins all had grenades and M16's. I had my Ithaca 12-gauge shotgun and 6 M61 grenades.

We quietly waited in ambush for the early morning, deep sleep hours. I threw the first grenade at 0200 hours and White opened up with the M60 raking the hootches. There was very little return fire. We had total surprise on our side.

The cleanup wasn't pretty. The VC had their girlfriends, wives, and families with them.

As I put holes in the boat hulls by firing buckshot from my shotgun into the boats, the squad destroyed all ordnance in the village and burned the hootches. The few survivors and children were allowed to go up the road to the next village. They could tell their stories about the Green Faces.

I called for our extraction.

The first SEAL killed in an active engagement was Billy Machen, PO-2 USN on August 16,1966. Billy Machen had attended the University of Texas from 1962 to 1965. He was on a recon mission about thirteen miles southeast of Nha Be along the Dinh Ba River. Machen was awarded the Silver Star, the nation's third highest medal for valor, posthumously. Most of us knew of him as a member of SEAL Team One's platoon operating south of Saigon.

My platoon knew that, so far, we had been very lucky.

CHAPTER 20

Operation Game Warden Continues

September 1966

There was another SEAL platoon operating out of Nha Be, the Naval Support Base on the Song Nha Be River about 8 kilometers (5 Miles) south of Saigon. SEALs brought the war to the enemy. Unlike conventional warfare firing artillery into coordinated locations, we operated close to our target. Combat was direct and often one on one. We brought a personal war to the enemy in what had been a safe area. SEALs had over 600 confirmed kills, another 300 most certainly killed, plus others that were captured and detained. The effect, including the psychological effect, was disproportional to our numbers. We had created an unspoken balance of terror and gained a reputation as fearsome and extraordinary warriors. We were winning the psychological war in the Rung Sat Special Zone.

I hadn't had a proper hot shower in almost a month. My boots were rotting out. Everyone in the platoon was fighting jungle rot on their feet and privates. I requested a leave for the platoon from Cdr. Zanke. The Mobile Support Team, Campbell and his PBR (Patrol Boat River) crew, would chauffer us to Nha Be where would all be given two day's leave to relax in Saigon and be re-fitted.

After a long, hot shower, fresh fatigues, and a trip to the corpsman for anti-fungal lotion, I was off to see the sights in Saigon. Priority number one was finding a cold beer. The hustle and bustle of Saigon was an affront to my senses after being so long in the delta. The hustle of the city and the hustle from the bar girls made me uncomfortable. I just never found Vietnamese women very attractive. I also felt that as an officer and supposed gentleman that I should not participate in supporting the local prostitues. Two cold beers and I was ready to go back. The guys weren't due back for 48 hours so I grabbed a ride back to Nha Be with a Marine Captain that I had met at the bar.

There was one road from Saigon to Nha Be. The VC regularly attacked traffic on the road and mined it at night. The mine sweepers usually cleared the road each morning, but no one wanted to be on the road after dark. We made the trip safely and I breathed more easily inside the relative safety of the Naval Support Base. I spent the rest of my 48-hour leave rounding up and cumshawing (borrowing permanently) supplies. I stashed everything I could find that we might need and stacks of 5.56x45mm ammo for our M16's, C4 explosives, and M61 grenades on Campbell's 30-foot PBR. I found a box of the new M67 grenades and managed to extricate them from the Chief Petty Officer in charge of the supple depot in return for a bottle of Jack Daniels.

The M67 fragmentation grenade replaced the M61. It contained 6.5 grams of composition B explosive and used a new M213 4 second fuse. I had heard that the practice of "cooking" a grenade (releasing the safety clip and holding the grenade briefly before throwing to reduce the chance of the enemy throwing it back) was just slightly safer with the M67 because the new fuse was more predictable.

After getting our cumshawed supplies stowed on the boat, I went to the open air amphitheater next to the base exchange where the movie tonight was "The Sons of Katie Elder" starring John Wayne and Dean Martin. After the movie, I turned in early to a clean, dry cot and slept 9 hours.

My platoon was back the next day before dark. The PBR crew were true sailors and most likely would drag in just before their leave expired at midnight. I reviewed the inventory of supplies and ordnance that I had stashed on the boat. Everyone wanted to handle and heft the new M67 grenades. Another night to enjoy a hot shower and a clean, dry cot.

We shoved off in the PBR after breakfast with a still hung over boat crew. Chief Campbell was at least in reasonable shape at the helm. I volunteered to help navigate by reading the river charts that he had marked for our trip back. The Gunners Mate, Posey, was in really bad shape and I was hopeful that we would not run into any incoming. Fortunately, he fell asleep on the deck and that had the added benefit of quieting his wise ass remarks. One of the tributaries that we needed to traverse was only about 50 meters wide. I was concerned about small arms fire from the shoreline.

A 7.62x39 mm round from an AK-47 could easily pierce the hull of the boat and, of course, anyone on board. The Chief also had some concern. He pushed the throttles full forward and we skimmed along at 28 knots using speed as a defense. I carefully scanned the shoreline for any movement. I breathed more easily when our base came into view.

Lt. Devers, the Marine platoon leader that we had worked with a few months ago, was now Captain Devers and the Marine Company

Commander. He welcomed us back as we off-loaded our supplies. He asked if I could join him when we finished. I had Guadanoli take over and I followed him to the command hootch.

Devers had worked with the CIA during the Phoenix Program that targeted VC for interrogation, torture, and execution. It was very effective, especially what they called "the Bell telephone hour" where electric wires were attached to sensitive body parts – male or female. Devers had intel that a village chieftain and VC sympathizer had been providing support to the NVA supply line to the Vietcong the area. He had staged a Marine attack using two platoons to level the village. Unfortunately, the key VC leadership had escaped the attack.

Our job was to locate and eliminate the future threat of them resuming the operation and to capture one or more of the VC leaders for interrogation. HQ had a good idea that they had retreated to an island in the mangrove swamp that was approachable only by river. It could easily be destroyed with helicopter gunships, but the powers that be wanted a captive or captives for interrogation and that's where we came into the picture.

Most SEAL operations were accomplished by a single squad operating independently. I agreed with the Captain that VC survivors were likely to be there on the Nipa Palm island until they could get word to the NVA further up river or sympathizers could reach them with transportation upriver. Guadanoli was sick with a stomach ailment. Probably from the Vietnamese food that he had consumed while on leave. I decided that his squad would stay in camp for the 2-3 days that we expected to be gone.

The MST (Mobile Support Team) had a "Skimmer", a small Boston Whaler that could transport up to 7 men into small waterways. Plenty of room for my 5-man squad and a two-man crew. If our map was accurate, we could insert from the Skimmer, close to the southeast edge of the small island that was covered with a thick grove of palm trees.

We spent a couple of hours getting our ourselves ready and reviewing the mission plan. Figuring that it would be about a 90-minute boat ride to our planned insertion point, I planned on shoving off at 1930 hours. Fortunately, it was an uneventful ride to the island. Close to our insertion point, Watson, PO-2 USN, our helmsman, throttled down to quietly idle the Skimmer in to the shore. We made our approach in the dark and waded onto the island. I could smell the gook fire up wind of us. We were that close. I took the point with my shotgun. Sneaking and peeking, we very slowly and quietly stalked the camp. I motioned for the squad to stop when I reached the edge of the clearing around the camp. I was 20 meters from the hootch that was just left or south of the smoky fire pit.

The nightly rain had assisted our quiet approach and there was no indication of alarm in the camp. As I was about to lob one of our new M67 grenades into the hootch, a gook came out ostensibly to take a leak. He walked straight toward me and when he reached 15 meters, I pumped two 12-gauge rounds of buckshot into him. The squad opened up on the hootch.

The CIA would not have the opportunity to interrogate, read torture, any survivors. The Green Faces just weren't trained to take prisoners. We survived by using surprise and accurate, overwhelming firepower.

Searching the four VC bodies, we found some handwritten documents in Vietnamese. We had eliminated the threat in a matter of hours. After burning the hootch and throwing the VC weapons into the river, we waded out to the Skimmer that I had called back. Our trip back to our base was thankfully uneventful. We were back at our base for a late shower. I filed my after action report before I turned in for the night.

As I was finishing breakfast the next morning, Sgt. Watson from HQ Company came up to me. He said, "Capt. Devers and Mr. DaSilva would like to see you, sir."

I ditched the rest of my coffee and rose to follow him as he mentioned,"Mr. DaSilva seemed a bit upset that you were unable to bring in any captives, sir."

"Thanks for the heads up, Watson."

The CIA chief could yell and scream all he wanted. I didn't report to him and my first priority was to my men. We had no casualties and we had eliminated the potential threat. To me that was a job well-done. I listened as DaSilva chewed my ass, but repeated what I had stated in my after action report that we had no opportunity to capture any of the VC leaders in the hootch. When DaSilva appeared to pause, Capt. Devers quickly dismissed me.

I heard later that afternoon that DaSilva had gone back to Saigon. I knew that he had effectively gotten intelligence that we needed and often relied upon, but he was a slimy bastard that I didn't have to like or respect.

We worked primarily with River Division 53 based in My Tho. After several missions with Chief Campbell and his PBR crew, we had confidence in their ability to insert and extract us from difficult spots on schedule. During Operation Game Warden the Navy was steadily consolidating forces around the Mekong Delta and destroying VC river supply lines by denying the use of the rivers to the VC. It was estimated that some 2,000 Viet Cong boats and river craft were destroyed and over 1,400 VC killed, wounded, or captured. Combined U.S. forces had suffered 39 killed in action.

On the radio, I heard that President de Gaulle of France gave a speech in Phnom Penh, Cambodia denouncing U.S. policy in Vietnam and urging our government to pull our troops out of Southeast Asia before more of our young men were killed. Of course, the stateside press picked up on this and spread the dis-information of our demise.

C H A P T E R   2 1

Training Mission

October 1966

A new guy, Jaros, Joseph K., PO-2 USN, joined us fresh from the states. The SEALs were upgrading to 6 man squads when possible. For the last two weeks, my two squads had alternated on what we called "Freak Out Missions". We would stalk and kill VC sympathizers. It was profound psychological warfare directed at the locals. We were being very effective as more Vietnamese began giving us information voluntarily on VC and NVA movements in the area. However, the powers that be decided that my platoon had a new calling.

We would be airlifted about 70 klicks to a spot along the Tien Giang River where there had been increased VC activity based on air reconnaissance. HQ wanted first hand intelligence on a suspected large supply point before calling in air strikes. They did not want to destroy friendlies and increase the negative media. Not the best use of a SEAL squad, but then the Army and CIA were calling the shots on this mission. There were an estimated 150-200 NVA and VC at the target supply depot.

129

My platoon and I were short-timers. We were counting our remaining days in-country before being rotated back to the states.

Four more weeks. I was going home with the rest of the team. One more mission, maybe. Think in the present tense, this mission, focus. Just a short patrol to reconnoiter. We were scheduled to be transported in by helicopter, a Bell UH-1 Iroquois would be waiting for us at 0 dark 30. The HU-1, powered by a single, turboshaft engine, with a two-bladed main rotor and tail rotor, was nicknamed the Huey. The Huey was the workhorse for the Army and Marine Corps and the two bladed rotor made a distinctive whoop-whoop that could be heard a long way off.

Airlifted in by Huey and then picked up a PBR (Patrol Boat, River) in the river. The PBR, a 31-foot fiberglass Uniflite made in Bellingham, Washington converted for river patrol, would pick us up tonight at 2200 hours. No problem, just do your job. If everyone did their job, we'd jump off just far enough east to be concealed, get a stealthy look at the VC supply depot a few kilometers south of Vinh Long, really just a spot of high ground where they cached supplies and ordnance; supply the verification of the coordinates to OPs and be out of there.

These concealed supply depots were a critical lifeline for the VC forces. Earlier, the main north-south conduit for trade had been the 1250-mile sinuous single track railroad running from Lang Son in the North just south of China through Hanoi to Saigon. The rail line crossed the Ben Hai River at the 17th parallel and continued through the former Demilitarized Zone (DMZ). As the 10,000-Day War grew in intensity, the section around the Gulf of Tonkin was pummeled around the clock by the bombers from the Navy, Air Force, Marines, and the Seventh Fleet off shore. Further south, the spectacular scenery from the Hai Van Pass to Da Nang became battle scarred, cratered and totally unpassable. The rails hug the coast along the South China Sea where the U.S. Marines landed at Red Beach on March 8, 1965. In desperation, the Viet Cong developed the Ho Chi Minh Trail, an ever changing network of roads and foot paths, and used trucks, bicycles and teenaged volunteers of either sex to ferry logistical supplies to their field units in the south.

Our drop was routine. All quiet along the northern side of the Tien Giang River. We had two hours to cover 5 kilometers to our target. We were about 50 miles northwest of where the river flowed into the South China Sea. This part of the country had quite a bit of high ground and we made good progress. Joe Guadanoli, Chief Petty Officer, USN, slowed us down with a hand signal. We were close to our target and stealth was in order. Moving quietly along the edge of what is called the Plain of Reeds was slow work and required unit focus. Sneaking and peeking.

We rotated the point position with Jaros. Murphy's Law, the new guy never saw the trip wire. Stealth and our reconnaissance mission went out with a blast. We stumbled into a platoon-sized encampment of gooks who had booby trapped the area before lighting their cooking fires. The VC cook had just started their early meal of Pho Ha Noi, a favorite noodle soup, when Jaros, our new guy, hit the wire. His legs were gone and his stumps pouring out his life blood. Damn. Now, I could smell the smoke. The heavy growth of the jungle had wafted the air currents around. We were in deep shit.

The two VC sentries took advantage of the initial noise and confusion, spotting us as we attempted to find cover. They concentrated fire on our exposed flank and Castanaro was hit. Our communications gear was blown to pieces with along with Geary, Joseph L., CPO-1. Castanaro was mobile, but bleeding badly from his upper left arm. Collins, Guadanoli and I opened fire and I signaled the squad to moved out. Like most firefights, it was over quickly. Now, we were the prey with no way of calling in air support.

We moved quickly toward a low lying section that we had skirted on the way in. Slipping into the covering slime of the mangrove swamp, we were safely ahead of the squad-sized group of gooks pursuing us. We set up our positions on some hummocks. The platoon knew the routine. With only hand signals, we staked out the killing field.

We didn't have to wait long. Our hidey spots went undetected as they the crept up to the edge of the slime. They were hunting us. The Ithaca Model 37 12-gauge pump shotgun with OO or double ought buckshot that was my constant companion would fire 8 rounds as fast as I could pump the action while holding down the trigger. It was a devastating close combat weapon that would fire clean or abused with filth. We were seasoned predators. We were ready to count coup as my Shoshone ancestors would say and later tell and re-tell the story around their evening campfires.

The VC crept and waded to about 10 meters in the undergrowth and then I could tell they smelled or sensed us. We were a bit ripe. It was difficult to keep that scent from wafting over the Rung Sat stink. The lead VC straightened a bit sniffing the air.

White nearly cut him in half with a short burst from his M60. Then all hell broke loose. My shotgun spit out a fast two rounds and the buckshot cut through the lush vegetation and dropped the number two guy. Collins lofted a grenade that took down a huddled group of three VC. There were three more wounded gooks writhing around. White finished them off. I knew that the rest of the VC platoon would soon be on our trail. Through hand signals, we disappeared into the swamp.

Three days later, Guadanoli, Collins, White, Rivera, Keane, Castanaro, Connell, Jones, and I walked into a TAC Support Unit. There were two good Americans back in the swamp and eight dead VC to accompany their spirits to the happy hunting ground. I was a good predator, the leader of the pack, a good Indian, but two of my platoon were dead or MIA.

I spent the next 2 hours with the 1st Battalion 3rd Marines HQ Company volunteering to go back with some air support to extract the rest of my platoon. I am indebted to Col. Mike Weston who commandeered the needed resources. My platoon all volunteered to accompany the Marines going back to retrieve my guys.

My platoon was now down to one squad plus. We went back with a platoon of Marines to mop up the VC's and retrieve the bodies of Geary and Jaros. After I cleaned my personal weapons, I showered and sat down to write my after action report and those dreaded letters to the next of kin.

Man, I got to change jobs.

CHAPTER 22

Two Weeks Left

October 1966

The remnants of my platoon had two weeks left in country. I was ordered to My Tho. We were to assist in training the Army of the Republic of Vietnam (ARVN) in guerilla warfare tactics and techniques.

After a short helicopter ride, courtesy of the U.S. Army, I reported in to my CO, Commander Alfred "Bud" Costello, United States Naval Academy class of 1957. Cmdr. Costello even knew Vice Admiral Draper Kauffman, father of the Navy's Underwater Demolition Teams. The UDT concept was later expanded from the frogman to the SEa, Air, Land (SEAL) combat team in 1958. Cross-trained in disciplines of the other services, President Kennedy realized in 1961 that highly trained, small units that were extremely mobile and self-sufficient in the boondocks could be very useful. The President directed that this unit be expanded into SEAL Team One and SEAL Team Two with further specialized training in reconnaissance (assisted by the Marine Corps, Forest RECON), jungle survival (Army, Ranger), and training with Army Airborne/ Special Forces.

The Cmdr. wanted to talk. Probably as a good CO, he understood my mental state. Cmdr. Costello knew the history of Vietnam. Previously, it had been three kingdoms. In the north were the industrious Tonkinese. South in the fertile Mekong delta rice bowl were the more laid back Cochinese and in the remote Annamese Cordillera mountain chain were various ethnic minorities, generally referred to as the Montagnards or Mountain People. The South China Sea was notorious for piracy and the sea ports were frequented by smugglers. Late in the 19th century the French saw Indochina as valuable real estate and colonized Vietnam developing extensive tea, coffee, pepper, and rubber plantations. Often, they indentured the backward and animistic ethnic tribes to work their plantations and to serve as mercenaries to guard against the ever expanding anti-colonial Vietminh. In the early 1950's with the Vietminh movement gaining more strength, the nascent army of a former history teacher, General Vo Nguyen Giap over ran the northern posts of France's crack Légion Étranger Parachutistes (Foreign Legion Paratroopers). It was in those northern mountains that Ho Chi Minh and resistance fighters took on the Japanese with help from the U.S. Office of Strategic Services, which later became the CIA. It was the beginning of the end of the French domination and resulted in partitioning the region into two countries, North and South Vietnam, by the Geneva Accords. Since 1954, the South Vietnamese could not, without extreme difficulty, visit their relatives or the graves of their ancestors in the north. A neutral International Control Commission had been established to control the border, the DMZ on the 17th parallel.

The Geneva Accords was a European solution that was hypothetically expedient. It cost Lt. Thomas E. Herndon, my spirt brother, everything he had and everything he might have been. I promised the great spirit that, when I got stateside, I would visit each of the families of my SEAL brothers and then my good friends the Herndon's, Tommy's parents, last.

I had fourteen more days in country and then thirty days of leave stateside.

Without a full team, my remaining team members were assigned to liaison duties with an ARVN (Army of the Republic of Vietnam) Ranger unit. The diminutive ARVN Rangers with their maroon berets were fighting for their country. They were good fighters, once engaged, and merciless with VC captives. The U.S. media had done them a huge disservice in reporting all the bad and little, if any, of the good. They were a dedicated, hard-bitten group on the front lines. For two weeks, I would do my best to help them with small unit guerilla tactics.

Major Tho Duc Nguyen, or Ted, was from Hue, an historically beautiful, coastal city known for its excellent cuisine. Ted was a patriot. Son of a college professor and a Ph.D. candidate in history before his country's call to duty. Ted was fighting for freedom and for his family. His English was adequate, but not fluent. I took an immediate liking to this quiet and competent young officer, who cared for and had the respect of his men. The ARVN needed more officers like Major Nguyen. Hell, so did we.

My easy couple of days to rotation didn't last. The ARVN Ranger unit got their orders to be part of the anvil in a classic hammer and anvil operation west of My Tho on the edge of the Plain of Reeds. I had been there on my first tour of duty and I suppressed the feelings that I had about returning to the high ground. It wasn't fear. I was now much more comfortable in the swamp than in the highlands. Instead of training the ARVN in guerrilla tactics, we were being used as an infantry unit. Collins, Guadanoli, White, Jones, and I were going back into action and we were going to count more coup for our fallen comrades. Castanaro had been medically evacuated. The other three guys were working with an ARVN river patrol unit.

It had been rumored that the South Vietnamese felt culturally inferior to the North. Early in our support of ARVN units the Army had found that their feelings made it difficult for the ARVN troops to enthusiastically engage in night operations. More importantly, it was found that in ambush situations that a small noise, the snick of a rifle action, a cough, or broken branch could tip off the approaching VC. In the South Vietnamese mind, he had just saved himself from sure death from the culturally superior North.

Major Ted and I decided that a short pep talk was in order before we disembarked.

Dark thoughts tried to creep into my consciousness as we went over the mission operations for the fourth time to make reactions automatic. I was a short-timer, but couldn't afford the luxury of dreaming about going home. Accomplish the mission and bring the troops back.

The ARVN Rangers were transported up river to Kien Phong. We then hiked due north to set up our position through a maze of levies built to irrigate the rice fields. Major Tho Duc Nguyen competently positioned his men to intercept the VC pushed by the U.S. Army IV Corps detachment acting as the hammer. Now came the hard part. Quietly wait in anticipation. Combat was characterized by long periods of semi-boredom followed by minutes of terrifying, violent activity. I was looking forward to the adrenaline high of combat that included improved eye focus and the ability to mentally slow down the high speed events that would take place. The humidity increased and the stench from the human fertilizer used on the rice paddies became overpowering. We waited.

The Major and I quietly reviewed and moved around checking the defensive positions and spoke encouraging words to the ARVN Rangers. Collins, Jones, White, and Guadanoli were reviewing the plan with the squad leaders and we waited some more. Hours went by and we waited.

As the afternoon shadows grew longer, a Douglas AC-47D Spooky flew over. Approaching the horizon, it began devastating everything on the ridge top east of our position. Nicknamed Puff the Magic Dragon, the AC-47D gunship (the military version of the DC-3) had been modified by mounting three MXU-470/A guns to fire through two rear window openings and the side cargo door, all on the left (pilot's) side of the aircraft.

The guns were actuated by a control on the pilot's yoke, where he could control the guns either individually or together, although gunners were also among the crew to assist with gun failures and similar issues. Spooky's primary function was close air support for ground troops. It could orbit the target for hours. Coverage given by a Spooky was over an elliptical area approximately 47 meters in diameter, placing a round every 2.2 meters during a 3-second burst. Each of its three 7.62 mm mini guns could selectively fire either 50 or 100 rounds per second. Cruising in an overhead left-hand orbit at 120 knots air speed at an altitude of 3,000 feet, the gunship could put a bullet or glowing red tracer bullet (every fifth round) into every square yard of a football field-sized target in potentially less than 10 seconds. The aircraft also carried flares, which it could drop to illuminate the battleground. Puff the Magic Dragon was airborne devastation to ground troops.

Over the horizon, Charlie was being harassed and he was being pushed straight to our position. Puff was pummeling Charlie as the VC and NVA troops crossed the ridge. We would intercept Charlie's escape to Cambodia. They would be pushed and killed by the hammer and then crushed by the anvil - us.

The backup was M109 heavy artillery that would cut loose to confuse, delay, and demolish Charlie as the they approached within 18 kilometers or about 11 miles. The M109 is an American-made self-propelled 155 mm howitzer, first introduced in the early 1960s. The M109 has a crew of six: the section chief, the driver, the gunner, the assistant gunner and two ammunition handlers. The gunner aims the cannon left or right (deflection), the assistant gunner aims the cannon up and down (quadrant). The M109 has a .50-caliber M2 machine gun as secondary armament.

Any VC that were still mobile and moving toward us, west toward Cambodia, were our targets. We were the anvil.

The artillery barrage began at 1700 and continued with the howitzer rounds progressively walking closer to us. They were coming.

In the growing darkness, we hunkered down and waited. I was reminded of how combat was hours of boredom followed by terrible minutes of trying to survive to fight another day.

A sentry called in movement detected about a klick to our southeast. The firefight broke out seconds later. Tracers were arcing into our position. Within 10 minutes it was quiet again.

After 20 minutes, I was about to suggest sending out a patrol to reconnoiter when the Major concluded that the majority of the VC had skirted our southeast position. We would not pursue them in the darkness. We had zero casualties and had counted no coup. The ARVN Rangers were joyous. Guadanoli reported in from his position with the platoon on the far northwest side. One of the ARVN Rangers had fired a round at movement well out of range giving away our position.

Setting our sentries, we slept in our dugout positions.

We were airlifted out the next morning. The IV Corps detachment had casualties. Disembarking from the helicopter, I passed the bodies stacked like cord wood and the pile of detached arms, legs and other parts sitting in the morning sun. I will always remember the smell of mangled, bloated, and rotting flesh.

I've often thought that when we elect a commander-in-chief that has not been in combat, we should find someplace in the world to our let our elected leader see and smell the aftermath of combat before he commits us to fight. After seeing the elephant, as the combat hardened say, I have to believe that our leaders would be far more reticent to commit our finest young men and women, if they only knew the terrible aftermath.

My after action report was succinct and tacit. I didn't burn Ted, but I alluded to the missed opportunity. Soon, I would be headed home or least to the good old USA. I assumed that a large number of my peers in the states still hated us for defending freedom.

With just a week left in-country, I thought that my platoon would be assigned routine duty close to My Tho. I still haven't learned to think like the brass. We got assigned to riverine duty. The VC river pirates were still at their nefarious activities between the South China Sea and the confluence of the Tien and My Tho rivers. Our job was to ride a Swift boat and assist the six-man crew in interdicting the pirates.

PCF-32 (Patrol Boat, Fast or PBF) commanded by LTJG Kellerstad, John Herman, USN, was the boat captain that we would ride along with on our support mission. In April 1966, PCF-32 arrived in Cam Ranh Bay from Subic on board the USS Catamount LSD-17. It was one of three PCF's under operational control of CTF116 for patrol in the Rung Sat Special Zone. Along with the boat captain, the crew consisted of a Boatswain Mate, Engineman, Radioman, and two gunners, usually a Gunners Mate and a Quartermaster.

We boarded PCF-32 for our first ride on the 51-foot Swift boat. We were headed down Song Cua Tien towards Phuoc Cung about 35 kilometers away on the South China Sea. It was reported that sampans and Vietnamese junks were interdicting shipping between there and Nha Be.

About an hour down the river, there is a fishing village, Vam Kinh, with a small beach where the brown river water washes the silt into shore at a bend in the river. Passing the beach, a B-40 rocket whooshed behind us and light small arms fire whistled around us.

The boat crew returned fire. Gunners Mate Merritt on the forward .50- caliber M2 Browning machine gun raked the beach. Quartermaster Stone loaded and began lobbing 81 mm mortars toward the tree line from the aft mortar mount. The Skipper headed to the beach. He nosed us into shallow water and we jumped in.

The boat crew provided covering fire as we charged up the beach to the tree line. The gooks ran for the jungle. Guadanoli and White had M60 7.62mm machine guns and three gooks didn't make the trees. The boat crew had accounted for two more. I never fired a shot. We searched the bodies, but found nothing of intelligence value.

The boat had some minor damage above the water line. Good luck was with us. No casualties.

The Skipper, LTJG Kellerstad, reviewed the dinged aluminum gunwales and a few small holes from the gun fire and ascertained that we would continue our mission. We slowly passed the village of Vam Kinh with its sampans and floating market. The villagers stood along the river bank and stared at us as we passed. Merritt stayed on the forward gun mount and trained the .50 caliber on the shore as we passed. We didn't receive any more incoming fire.

We cruised another 25 minutes down river toward Phuoc Cung before overtaking a slow moving junk headed for the South China Sea. The Skipper maneuvered the PBF near the port bow of the junk and motioned them to stop. Gunners Mate Merritt on the forward gun mount kept them covered. As the Skipper and I had previously discussed, my squad prepared to board the junk to search it from stem to stern.

Just as I prepared to board the junk over the port side, the gooks threw some things over the starboard side of the junk out of our view. I heard the splashes and jumped on board followed by White, the very large, black Marine in my squad.

White was a very intimidating 6 foot 5 inches built like an NFL lineman and towered over me – and I'm not really small. The average gook was more like 5 feet 4 inches and 140 pounds. The 6-man crew of the junk raised their hands in surrender.

The rest of the squad boarded and began searching the junk as White and I covered the crew. I was pretty sure that they had tossed firearms and possibly rockets overboard. We had a surprise when Rivera came up on deck herding two gooks that been hiding below.

The Skipper called in to My Tho HQ and the Unit Commander ordered us to bring in the captured junk and crew of suspected pirates. He had special interest in the two VC that were hiding below decks. As Boatswain Mate Wilkins and Quartermaster Stone came onboard the junk to pilot it back to My Tho, we secured the gooks and would ride back on the junk to keep them out of mischief. It was a slow ride upriver in the junk with LTJG Kellerstad keeping the PBF close behind. We had the gooks tied and seated in the stern of the junk and I was facing them sitting on a box covering them with my shotgun across my lap. Right behind us was the Swift boat with its .50 caliber machine guns pointed right at us. It was more than a little disquieting for me looking at the Browning .50 caliber trained on us.

CHAPTER 23

Going Home

November 1966

My last day in-country finally came and was thankfully uneventful. I hitched a ride on a Chinook into Saigon filled with 10 body bags, all Marines, to be processed for shipment home. The Boeing Chinook CH-47 is the medium lift workhorse of the helicopter fleet. Tan Son Nhut airport with its dilapidated terminal and cold beer was a welcome sight. The heat radiating off the tarmac was like a furnace even in the forenoon. I didn't care. I was scheduled on a MATS flight leaving this afternoon and eventually to the United States. Home.

Thirty-four hours later I stepped off the plane at NAS (Naval Air Station) Alameda, adjacent to Oakland, California and about six miles southwest of the University of California at Berkeley. Culture shock.

Cmdr. Vanderbeck at NAS Alameda asked if I could address the Midshipman in the NROTC Program at the University of California at Berkeley. He said that it would be good for them to get some inside information on the SEALs mission in Southeast Asia and insight into the whole SEAL program. The next day, I was visiting the University of California, Berkeley in dress blues. Three and a half days out of the swamp and invited to speak to the NROTC (Naval Reserve Officers Training Corps) at CAL (all ROTC was later disbanded temporarily by the college as not politically correct).

Pretty, sun tanned, young girls screamed ugly epithets at me when I got out of the cab at the intersection of Bancroft and Bowditch Streets. I walked to the ROTC unit located at 152 Hearst Gymnasium. I reported in to Captain Malcolm Roderick, USN, Commanding Officer, NROTC at UC Berkeley. After my short talk about the teams and small unit operations, I fielded far too many questions about what it was like in-country, how tough was training in Coronado, and Hell Week before SEAL graduation. Stopping for some coffee at the student union after an hour and a half with the clean cut, fresh faces of the soon to be commissioned young men of the NROTC unit, I scanned the Oakland Tribune. Even the newspapers got to me. The grungy flower children were everywhere as I walked back to find a cab on University Avenue. My mind exploded, but I maintained control - sort of. The long haired, scruffy guys with the pretty, sun tanned girls gave me some space. Probably because I was in shape and out weighed them considerably, but maybe because they read something in my eyes. The thousand-yard stare. They will never know how close to annihilation they came. Thankfully, nobody spit on me.

Man, I've got to change jobs.

Some debriefing. The cold sweat ran down my back as I sat in the cab riding back to Alameda NAS. The Navy was a part of me. The only friends I had were guys that I'd served with over the past six years or before that at the University of Texas. Only there were fewer of them now than back then. Vietnam took the best and most dedicated of my peers. It wasn't fair.

The absolute fatigue after combat, the physical exertion of patrols and the exhilaration of surviving a firefight made sleeping tolerable in-country. Now, back on home soil, I could not sleep. The BOQ (Bachelor Officers Quarters) was too serene and I was not physically exhausted. The images from Berkeley were too strong. The virus of hatred kept me awake as I tried to evaluate and rationalize. I knew it wasn't fair and never would be. The best and the brightest were being sacrificed to protect the Black Panthers, the draft dodgers that ran away to Canada, the celebrities who made millions while helping to motivate our enemies to kill and mutilate more of my brothers.

About 0430, I made the decision to fulfill my pledge and visit the families of my brothers and then, finally, go to Austin, Texas and visit Tommy's grave. Three days later after visiting Boston, Columbus, and Houston I was ready to visit Austin. Calling ahead to Tommy's parents, I told them my plans. Tommy's Dad, Chet, offered to pick me up at the airport and insisted that I stay with them at the ranch.

I spent an awkward day with the Herndon's. Tommy's kid sister Carole was happily married in New York and now had her first child on the way. My heart was still broken, but I knew there never was a chance for me with Carole. Afterwards, I didn't quite know what to do next. So, I went home to Wyoming.

CHAPTER 24

Pinedale, Wyoming

December 1966

Things hadn't changed much in Pinedale. The guys that I had played ball with in high school were still there. Drinking at the pub and re-telling old stories. The cheer leaders were heavier, no longer fresh-faced and attractive, and most had several kids. I had one beer with the guys and tactfully excused myself. My afternoon walk took me by the high school. I could still see the light on in Dr. Moran's office, the Guidance Counselor that convinced me to accept the Navy scholarship instead of accepting the real money offered to me to play minor league baseball. In retrospect, he had convinced me to find a life in the outside world. His learned perspective and more global view were needed once again. He gave me a warm welcome and seemed genuinely glad to see me again. After a while, I told him about my Berkeley experience. He assured me that it was not representative behavior in Pinedale or most of middle America, regardless of what was reported on TV. But I had seen it up close and personal.

Dr. Moran then asked, "What are your plans, now? Are you going to make a career of the Navy?"

"I really don't know. I'm confident of my ability and decision-making in combat, but I have not seriously considered what else I can do. I'm a good warrior, but really have few civilian skills. The reality is that I trust and respect the men that I have served with and I feel like I'm part of the team."

I hadn't known that Dr. Moran had served in Korea and used the GI Bill to get his graduate degrees. He spoke earnestly about his service as a young lieutenant in the infantry. He walked with a cane now because of an injury to his left foot. He told me that he had been wounded at the Battle of the Chosin Reservoir in Korea back in December of 1950. He spoke of the men that he trusted implicitly in combat and that since then, in civilian life, he considered himself very fortunate to have three close friends that he could rely upon.

He talked about graduate school as a way for me to gain a marketable skill set. Skills that could apply to a career in civilian life and also increase my future value to the Navy. He rustled through a stack of papers on his desk and mentioned that the Graduate Record Exams were being conducted soon and I should consider taking them while I'm home on leave. The next exam anywhere nearby was scheduled to be administered in Cheyenne, some 350 miles from Pinedale, but Dr. Moran offered to assist me over the next two weeks in preparing for the test. Dr. Moran also knew about a Navy program for selected officers to attend graduate school while remaining on active duty with pay and benefits. Dr. Moran suggested that I apply for the program and apply to an East Coast university for a less controversial student body.

I knew I couldn't stay in Pinedale. I cherished Mom and Dad, but couldn't stay and the Navy was now my home. Calling the SEAL base in Coronado, I had a conversation with Cmdr. Kaufman. He knew my record and immediately said that he would look into the graduate school program. With typical efficiency, the Commander's Chief Yeoman got back to me the following Monday with a good to go. I would receive orders to attend an accredited master's degree program at one of the affiliated NROTC colleges of my choice for a period not exceed two years. Not only would I continue to receive compensation at my current pay grade of O-3 and all benefits, but the Navy would pay my tuition. I was granted extended leave. The Navy was taking care of their own. I would be forever grateful.

The test results weren't due until January 3rd and I was concerned about getting admitted anywhere at this late date for a mid-term entry. I was fidgety. My Dad helped by taking me on long walks behind Burnt Lake where we would enjoy the solitude along the continental divide and catch a few trout through the ice. He never asked about 'Nam or what I did there. We often spent hours in that gorgeous country without a spoken word, but I could read the joy in his eyes to have me home and with him.

Somehow Dr. Moran pulled the right strings. My exam scores were in the top 95th per centile and I was accepted for an unusual entrance for the spring semester at Northeastern University in Boston. Dr. Moran received his PhD there. His former classmate, Dr. Friedlander, was now President of Northeastern. I suspect strongly that there had been some conversation about my atypical admission. I thanked Dr. Moran for all his help and his one-on-one cramming with me for the Graduate Record Exam.

Thanks to the Navy plus meager savings from my days in-country I had adequate financial security and could afford a few luxuries. I traded in my old '56 Mercury for a new Ford Galaxy 500 convertible in midnight blue. I headed off for graduate school in Boston. It was much calmer on campus than what I had witnessed in California. The other students at the Northeastern really didn't care nor did they have much time to wonder about anyone's previous life. I had let me hair grow out so that I was not as conspicuous.

After SEAL training, business school was pretty straight forward. Put in the study time, organize, and be prepared. The time flew by and I did well, especially in the verbal rough and tumble of the case studies. My classmates soon found out that I was not easily intimidated by rhetoric. I read the Wall Street Journal everyday dawdling over breakfast to help prepare for my finance class. I had some savings in a CD or Certificate of Deposit that had just matured and I decided to open a margin account at Merrill Lynch to put my new found understanding of financial analysis to work.

The kid assigned as my broker, Andy Northrup, was smooth and articulate, but seemed years younger than me. We were both twenty-seven. Andy had a degree in business administration from the University of Virginia and had worked for Xerox as an account executive for four years selling copiers. Last year, he said that he saw the light and became a stock broker, so he could help guide people with their investments. He sounded very sincere as he told me about his calling to help his clients invest their life savings for a better future. He asked very little about me. Andy said that it was too bad that I got drafted into 'Nam; that maybe now that I was home I could get my career started. He was most interested in how much I thought that I could invest. I didn't bother to fill him in on my background and that I had not been drafted.

As I filled out the forms required by Merrill Lynch to open a new account, my new broker explained hypothecation, street name, margin buying, and commodities futures in a perfunctory manner using all the trade jargon that he had been taught. There was no reason to tell him that my last project at the Business School had been constructing an econometric model of options trading and that I felt competent enough on general market issues to think that I could successfully pass the test for a Series 7 license. He was doing his job peddling and I didn't need to assuage my ego. I filled out the forms and signed over the cashier's check for $21,000 that I had received from the bank after cashing in my matured CD. I wished him well in his new career and bought 200 shares of IBM, ignoring his muted pitch on the utility industry.

I really didn't want to go home that first summer, so I took extra classes and worked nights as a martial arts instructor at the Tae Kwon Do Academy. It kept me in shape and gave me some pin money. I spent my days in class or at Fenway Park, just a short walk from the Huntington Avenue campus, watching the Red Sox. The Wall Street Journal had become part of my daily ritual and the extra money from my job as an instructor allowed me to begin systematically investing in some companies that my professors used as examples in our course work and case studies. I enjoyed the research and analysis and began to understand both technical and fundamental investing approaches. The months flew by. I guess I really enjoyed my almost two years in Boston. At least, nobody was shooting at me and I no longer had those dreadful letters to write.

My financial analysis proved spot on and my stock portfolio was comfortably in six figures and growing upon receiving my Master's in Economics. I paid off the mortgage on my parents' house after they came to my graduation. Many of my classmates were going to work for Wall Street hedge funds and big-time consulting firms for large salaries. Dad asked me what were my plans. Easy answer, I was still Lt. Stryker, USN. The team was family and the Navy had taken good care of me. The anti-war sentiment was growing and being fueled by a left wing press. I knew that we were consistently beating the NVA and VC in firefights and our kill ratio was around 10 to 1. South Vietnamese were fighting for their freedom and we had agreed to support them.

It shouldn't have been a surprise that government agencies actively recruited the new graduates. The CIA recruiter was ex-Navy and knew quite a bit about my military record. Someone had done some research and it felt good to be wanted. Deep inside, I still felt that I owed the Navy for getting me out of Pinedale and now with a master's degree. The Navy had a good program and they had gotten this Indian out of the mountains. Yeah, I still owed them. While the SOG (Special Operations Group) with the CIA was attractive, I was still Lt. Stryker, USN.

Dad understood that the blood of our forbearers flowed in my veins. I still had coup to count.

C H A P T E R   2 5

Reporting In

June 1, 1968

Following graduation, I took two weeks to drive from Boston to San Diego in my midnight blue Ford convertible. I stopped at historical sites along the way. I spent some time touring the National Air Force Museum in Dayton, Ohio and the Air Force Museum in Lincoln, Nebraska where I actually got to sit in the cockpit of an SR-71. The high altitude stealth plane like the one Gary Powers flew over the Soviet Union and was shot down. I followed the Oregon Trail to Kearney, Nebraska. Then went south to Denver and across the divide to Grand Junction. Then I went south to St. George, Utah. I spent three days in Las Vegas. Everyone should witness Las Vegas at least once. After losing $500 at the recently remodeled Caesar's Palace learning how not to play craps, it was time to head to San Diego and report in to Coronado. It was about a 5-hour drive and I decided to take the scenic route through Twentynine Palms, California, the site of the Marine Corps Air and Ground Combat Center. I took Route 95 south to Rice Road. The road had cattle crossings and little hills that almost got me airborne at 70 miles per hour. It was a nice drive through the Mojave Desert and then on to Route 10 through the San Bernardino Valley.

Crossing the bridge from San Diego to Coronado Island, I felt like I was coming home. Cmdr. Kaufman was still in charge. Chief Yeoman Thurman F. Monckton was the "Big Chief" at Coronado. Like all Navy chiefs. he got things done and knew what had to be done. The Commander was in a meeting and the Big Chief asked me to have a seat. I was officially still on leave. Chief Monckton proceeded to bring me up-to-date.

I found out that my old platoon had been scattered around with new assignments. Chief Guadanoli was an instructor at Camp Pendleton training new SEAL recruits, but was available for re-assignment. Collins retired from the Navy after 20 years of service. He had entered the Navy at age 17. Petty Officer 1st Class Jones was back in country with SEAL Team One. SSgt. White was convalescing from wounds received on his third tour of duty and had received the Navy Cross, the nation's second highest medal for valor under fire. He had also been promoted to Gunnery Sergeant. Collins, Molinari, and Larson were still active, but he would have to determine their whereabouts.

The Big Chief told me that it was not in the Navy's Rule Book to return to base early. He could get me orders if I chose to stay until my leave was actually up in three days. He strongly suggested that I explore San Diego and the beaches along the coast for awhile. I could just as easily report in to the Commander on June 4th when my leave was officially up.

I had learned long ago to always listen to the Navy Chief Petty Officers. I checked into BOQ (Bachelor Officers Quarters), packed three changes of civilian clothes, and two bathing suits, then headed out.

Southern California has one of the world's most perfect climates. Warm, sunny days with miles of beaches and the blue Pacific Ocean. I drove north about 25 miles on the Pacific Coast Highway Route 101 to Cardiff-By-the-Sea just south of Encinitas. There's a lagoon at the river's mouth where the surfers congregate. I hadn't cut my hair back to a half inch yet and figured I could lay on the beach and catch some rays without a hassle.

Parking at the public lot, I used the men's restroom to change into a bathing suit. I walked onto the beach and watched the surfers and beach beauties. One was strolling by along the edge of the wet sand.

She caught my I eye immediately. Tall and slim with strawberry blonde hair, she moved like an athlete. I was staring and she knew it.

Embarrassed, I could only manage to say, "Hi".

"Hi, yourself", she said and continued to stroll down the beach.

I was tongue tied and just watched her walk away. Later, I told myself what an idiot I was. Two hours later after a swim in the Pacific I still had a vision of her. That's all I had, no name or contact information. I was getting hungry so I headed back to Cardiff-By-the-Sea Lodge, where I had reserved a room, to shower and change for dinner. Just south of the San Elio Lagoon is restaurant row that I had driven by on my way into town. I remembered seeing a Chart House and decided a fish dinner would be appropriate.

The Chart House wasn't very busy. I was seated almost immediately upon arriving at a table by the window looking out over the Pacific and the setting sun. Unbelievably, my waitress was the stunning strawberry blonde from the beach.

She said, "Hello, again. My name is Jess. Can I get you a drink?"

"Hi, I'm Jack. I'd like an Absolut Vodka on the rocks with olives."

She efficiently disappeared to get my drink before I could get another word out. For someone who was used to giving orders and opinions, I was being a real goof ball.

Jess returned with my vodka and suggested the crab stuffed shrimp cooked on a cedar plank. I was watching how her blue eyes sparkled with life above the freckles on her nose. At that moment, I would have agreed with just about anything that she said and ordered the stuffed crab.

It was early for the dinner crowd and the restaurant was not yet very busy. Jess had time to wander over to my table. I managed to ask a dumb opening question, "Are you from here?"

Jess giggled, "No, I'm from San Diego. After I graduated from San Diego State last month, I decided to spend the summer at the beach. I work here six nights a week and spend my days catching rays and waves."

"Sounds like you've planned a great summer. What's next? What was your major?"

Some folks had just been seated by the maître de and Jess had to go greet them. After taking their drink orders, she returned with my entrée.

"To answer your question", she said, "I majored in psychology and I'm going to law school in September. I've been accepted at Hastings in San Francisco. I just need to get away from the military presence in San Diego."

Boy, did that comment set me back. I just replied, "Oh, well I'm in the Navy based in Coronado".

Jess got very busy elsewhere. After I finished my crab which was excellent, the table was bussed by a young Hispanic man. Jess came by with the check and did not say a single word. I was not asked if I wanted dessert. I got the message.

I left enough money on the table to give Jess a decent tip. I stopped at a raucous surfer bar on my way back to the lodge. Two more Absolut Vodka's and I would sleep at least six hours until dawn.

Up at first light, I went for a nice long run on the beach. There is something special about the running along the edge of the surf at daybreak. I ran south from the lagoon for 20 minutes and then did an about face and ran back. I didn't need to report in until the day after tomorrow, but I decided that I would rather be on the base in Coronado than out here with the undisciplined civilians. I drove back to the lodge, showered, and packed. I paid my bill and then put down the convertible top for the drive down the coast.

CHAPTER 26

Back in the Saddle

June 3, 1968

After reporting back in, I spent the afternoon catching up on things. The Tet Offensive had been launched at the end of January 1968 by the North Vietnam People's Army and the Vietcong by staging a number of surprise attacks in the Army I and II Corps Tactical Zones. Some 80,000 communist troops attacked more than 100 towns including 36 provincial capitals. It was the largest offensive to date. During the intense fighting the communists gained temporary control of several cities and executed thousands of people. Fighting around Khe Sanh continued into March. Although the communists suffered a severe military defeat, the news media reporting had a profound effect on the U.S. public. Public support of the war declined even further and the public sentiment urged politicians to seek negotiations to end it.

Peace talks had commenced in Paris and the North Vietnamese began Phase II of the Tet Offensive referred to as "Mini-Tet" in May 1968 ostensibly to enhance their bargaining position. The communists launched another attack on Saigon on 25 May. Viet Cong forces occupied six Buddhist pagodas in the mistaken belief that they would be immune from artillery and air attack. On June 18th 152 members of the Viet Cong's *Quyet Thang* Regiment surrendered to ARVN forces, the largest communist surrender of the war.

During the Tet Offensive, the Eighth Platoon of SEAL Team Two had assisted Army Special Forces at Chau Doc about 250 kilometers west of Saigon on the Cambodian border. The Platoon Officer-in-Charge Dick Marcinko led his team in an urban street battle that turned into a rescue mission. They saved American nurses and a school teacher trapped in the city. The news media in the good old USA made our victories look and sound like we were consistently losing.

The war continued and I had a good idea that I would be back in the Rung Sat before long.

The next day I received my orders. As Officer-in-Charge of the Third Platoon, I sat in HQ for the morning reviewing personnel folders of my new platoon that I would meet tomorrow. It was a nice surprise to have two squad leaders that had previously served with me. Two tried and true predators – Chief Guadanoli and Gunnery Sergeant White. White was just deemed medically fit to return to active duty and was enroute from Colorado.

The other 10 men had recently completed training, some had been under Guadanoli's watchful eyes during BUD/S. I felt comfortable again being with my brothers.

After meeting my new platoon, we would spend three days up at Camp Pendleton training for insertions and extractions by helicopter. While the majority of SEAL operations were conducted after inserting from river boats, it was in Vietnam that SEALs first began developing hit-and-run air-assault tactics using Army and

Navy helicopters. Operations involved helicopters in "slick" or passenger configurations, but were also lightly armed with door guns. We practiced inserting in heavy cover by dropping down lines while the Slick hovered above the canopy covering us with its door guns.

We were being prepared for operations in the Central Highlands as well as the Rung Sat Special Zone.

Upon our return to Coronado, I had the opportunity to meet Theodore Roosevelt IV, great-grandson of President Theodore Roosevelt, graduate of BUD/S 36. He had just returned from 'Nam and was headed back east.

I got our orders for my Third Platoon. We were headed to Da Nang. Da Nang is on the South China Sea at the mouth of the Han River. It was a major port city with a large airport. It has a tropical monsoon climate with two seasons. The dry season runs from April to September with daily high temperatures in the 90's Fahrenheit with high humidity and some thunder storms.

Landing, again, at Saigon's Ton Son Nhut airport, we had a couple of hours to kill before catching a flight on a C-130 to Da Nang. We found some shade and lukewarm beer thanks to the U.S. Air Force that ran the airport administration. We were to catch up with the 7th Marines that had been operating in hills west of Da Nang.

Sitting on the floor of the C-130 on the flight to Da Nang, Guadanoli, who had previously been in the area of Hill 327 in what was called the Oklahoma Hills, gave us an idea of the terrain that we would be operating in. The hills were about 15 kilometers west of Da Nang. It became increasing more mountainous traveling west toward Laos. It was heavily forested and rose a couple thousand feet above sea level. There were places where the forest canopy was so thick that the sun light didn't penetrate leaving the forest floor damp with rotting vegetation. The river valleys had heavy morning fog. Unlike the Rung Sat Special Zone, we would mostly be on solid ground.

Dropping down through the gathering dark clouds, we landed in Da Nang. The afternoon thunder storm was just starting. I had to find the 1st Battalion, 7th Marines commanding officer, Lt. Col. Fagan, somewhere west of Da Nang. I asked a Corporal after we disembarked the C-130 and he pointed me to the Marine Headquarters Company. I told Guadanoli to find the nearest A/C and have our Radio Man turn on the communications gear. I would find Headquarters Company then call him. White offered to take my gear. The big man could easily carry another 70 pounds.

The thermometer on the side of the hanger read 93 degrees. I guessed the relative humidity to be close to 90. At least there was a little breeze from the east off the China Sea.

Finding the HQ Company, Sgt. Pierce at the front table directed me to Capt. Head, the Company Commander, who introduced himself.

"Captain, I'm Lt. Stryker, SEAL Team One 3rd Platoon, Officer-n-Charge. My orders are to report to Lt.Col. Fagan. Can you direct me to him?"

"Welcome Lt. We've been expecting you. How many men are with you?"

"Captain, I have two squads of 6 men each with me and a Radio Man. Total of 14 men. We travel light and could squeeze into two Slicks."

Capt. Head excused himself and called for transport availability. Returning he said, "The Colonel is at a new Marine base camp being established on Freedom Hill west of here. There is a Chinook being loaded that can take your platoon out there now so you can set up your hootches. Headquarters Company will be moving there tomorrow. When you exit HQ, look north and you will have the Chinook in sight."

Our call sign was Golf-3 and I asked the Captain for permission to have Sgt. Pierce call Guadanoli to meet me at the Chinook.

CHAPTER 27

Freedom Hill

June 19, 1968

It was Wednesday. We had been on Freedom Hill for two days. We had some help from the Combat Engineers and were settled into our newly constructed hootches next to Officers Country, the group of hootches for the officers of 1ˢᵗ Battalion 7ᵗʰ Marines. To the east was the landing area and supply depot. The 7ᵗʰ Marines, Delta and Echo Companies, were South. Basically, we had a relatively safe position near the center of the camp and were close by HQ Company.

The mountainous region west of Da Nang harbored infiltration routes and major enemy base camps. From the Laotian border, supplies and men followed Highway 614 east. The supply route divided west of Song Con with one route following 614 to the Happy Valley and the other followed the river south to Song Yang then northeast to Thuong Duc then east along the Song Vu Gia River. The Marines had named the mountains to the west the Oklahoma Hills and they were infested with NVA and Vietcong. There were nightly 122mm rocket attacks on the Da Nang Vital Area. The VC launched their rocket attacks along a semi-circle from Marble Mountain in the south to the Hai Vau Pass in the north. Observation helicopters went out daily to locate the launch sites.

Our job would be to interdict the infiltration routes by waging guerilla warfare against the VC to psychologically soften them up for the Marines. I thought my platoon could do more than psychological terror. We were trained predators and I also wanted to locate and destroy the materiel caches and base camps that could mitigate the nightly mortar attacks.

The Oklahoma Hills were heavily forested and 2,000-3,000 feet high. Guadanoli's squad would be inserted near the terminus of Highway 614 in the Happy Valley. They would then disrupt the supplies coming down Highway 614. White's squad would go with me to Hill 52 near the village of Ha Nha along the Song Vu Gia River where we would interdict the other branch of the supply route. Our intent was to shut down or at least slow down the logistical supply lines coming in from Laos. We took our 3 day packs loaded with MRE's and as much ammo as we could carry. I had learned that I could go without a change of clothes and just about everything else except water, food, and ammo.

At 06:30 it promised to be a beautiful, hot sunny day in the middle of the wet season. We boarded a Slick that would insert us about a klick northeast of Song Vu Gia. As I sat in the doorway with my feet resting on the skid, the forest canopy below looked impenetrable as we skimmed above it. I had absolute confidence in my platoon. We would disrupt the NVA supply line and instill the worm of doubt into their future planning and recruitment in the local villages.

I got a tap on my shoulder and White pointed ahead at the opening in the forest where we would be inserted. It looked peaceful and I was hopeful that we could be quietly inserted to disappear in the forest. The helicopter pilot, Foster, Steven, WO-1 USA, manipulated the Slick into the small clearing with a skill that was exemplary. There was not more than 5 meters of clearance for the rotors.

As my feet hit the ground, a couple of rounds buzzed by me and shattered some plexiglas on the Huey. The squad scrambled for cover as Foster roared out of the clearing with the door gunner providing cover for us. The door gunner raked the brush and the incoming fire stopped. White's M60 fire was just insurance that the two dead gooks were no longer a threat.

There was a trail that lead northwest and since the dead gooks had most likely come running down that trail after hearing the Huey's distinctive whoop of the rotors, I signaled to White to parallel the trail. I expected more gooks to be exploring the sounds of our short firefight soon.

Moving into the forest, White motioned to Castanaro to take the point The forest floor under the canopy was damp and quiet which suited our sneaking and peeking approach. We were slightly above the trail and about 15 meters north of it. After 15 minutes, we had traveled only about 50 meters in the forest when Castanaro held up his arm to halt the squad. Couching down I could make out movement on the trail approaching our position.

Six gooks in traditional black pajamas carrying AK's came double timing along the trail. Molinari was our last in line and had an opening. He held out an M67 grenade and cooked it before tossing it in front of the lead gook. After the blast, my squad quickly dispatched the survivors with controlled fire. Searching for useful intel was fruitless. These weren't NVA officers or even VC leaders, but our LZ was most likely close to a VC camp and we needed to become ghosts in the forest.

Our good luck was holding.

I made an educated guess that the VC camp was down in the valley near the river, so we headed up the hill. Our morning's work would leave an impression and we could skirt the gook encampment and disrupt the supply line further west. Cresting the top of the hill there was a small opening in the forest canopy. I could see smoke from the village down below us. The VC camp could be a target of opportunity for any available aircraft in the area. I called in the coordinates and we moved out to interdict the supply route to the west.

We had traveled about a kilometer west when the explosions behind us indicated that the VC camp was being bombed. Another one for the home team. It was a very good day. Time to find a secluded spot to have an afternoon siesta to rest up for night's work. It was the early evening hours when the VC would be moving into their positions to prepare for the evening mortar attacks.

The narrow valleys and steep terrain made it very slow going and we had to ration our water supply in the heat. We found a protected place for our afternoon siesta. Since I needed to call in to HQ, I volunteered to take the first watch. I heard that Guadanoli's squad had located and destroyed a materiel cache and the 6 gooks guarding it. Guadanoli would continue working west to Song Con where we would hopefully meet for extraction.

It had been an all-around good day, so far.

1830 hours and time to review our evening plan. After a cold meal, we would move out to the west paralleling the river toward An Dien. We had intel from a defector that supplies were diverted from there to Base Area 112 and north into Charlie Ridge, the 10-mile-long chain of mountains west of Da Nang. Molinari took the point to pick our way back to the trail just south of us. White brought up the rear as we went single file in the growing darkness.

I had learned to prefer night operations. A small group could strike and then disappear. A night raid, especially between 0200 and 0400, by an adversary that disappeared into the gloaming had maximum psychological effect. Nearly all the VC villages had dogs that supplied them with an early warning system, pets, and food. Dog meat was a staple. Since we went days in high heat and high humidity without showers except the rain, the village dogs could smell us from far off.

The bright, three-quarter moon due this evening when the afternoon rain passed would allow us to move at a good, but careful pace tonight. At 2030 hours, I signaled for the squad to take a break. Chief White reviewed the map with me. It was a handwritten map that had been retrieved from a VC defector. I had used captured VC maps in the Rung Sat Special Zone that detailed every trail and creek. I had reasonable confidence that this map was a reasonably accurate representation of the terrain and local villages. There was a small village southwest of us on Route 4. The road that basically followed the Song Vu Gia River and was a main supply route. The river had a bend that brought it very near Route 4 in the An Hoa Valley.

It looked like a prime suspect for a VC supply cache of materiel coming in from Laos. It was our next target.

After a half-hour break, we saddled up with Larson on point. We found a small foot or bicycle trail that took us on a winding descent into the valley. We moved at a slow, steady pace on the lookout for booby traps. After about an hour, the updraft from the valley floor smelled of smoke wafting up from the evening fires in a village below us. Our point man Larson held up his hand to halt our progress.

White gave us the stay sign as he and Larson moved up to check out the village.

It is more difficult to wait than to sneak and peek reconnoitering a target. The minutes dragged on. Without knowing the exact position or makeup of the village there was no choice but to sit quietly, even a cough potentially could be heard at this distance by one of the village dogs.

Two quiet, slow moving shadows approached our position. White and Larson were back. White whispered, "Lt. the village is on the north side of the road only about 150 meters from here. The river is close to the south side of the road and there are five small boats tied up. There is an obvious cache of supplies just west of the last hootch. I think that we can booby trap both the east and west road exits without detection if we stay at 100 meters from the village because the road curves on both ends."

"Sounds good to me. Take three men to the west. I'll take the rest of the squad to fix the east end. Let's meet up at the ridge that we crested earlier then call in coordinates for an airstrike to hit village."

Moving quietly in the night we set up grenade traps on the road and staggered on each side. We retreated uphill without the village dogs barking and telegraphing our presence. White was waiting for us at the ridge. They had covered the west end without detection. While the VC would be delayed for awhile, I needed to call in an airstrike to preferably hit right after first light. We would stay here and observe the strike and mop up stragglers if needed.

"This is Golf-3 supply cache is at coordinates 278028. We have plugged the east and west exit routes on Route 4. In position and will hold."

Captain Head acknowledged and it was now time for a short nap before dawn. Molinari had the watch. I checked my weapons, took inventory of my ammo, and water. We had used all of our grenades setting traps and, then, I settled back using my pack for a headrest and my poncho as a blanket.

It was June 21, 1968, the squad was having breakfast when we heard the first explosions. Two Marine Corps F-4 Phantoms hedge hopped up the An Hoa Valley. Love those Marine Corps pilots. They came in low and fast. The village erupted and they were in their power climb before we actually heard the roar of their twin jet engines. They dropped their bombs and then came back around and strafed the village with their M61 Vulcan Gatling Cannons.

There were several muffled blasts. Our booby traps were working as some of the VC were evacuating the burning village. We moved carefully down the hill to mop up any survivors, capture documents, and blow up any ordinance or logistical supplies that survived the air attack. Fifty meters from the village I could hear the wailing of survivors and barking dogs over the roar of the remaining fires.

I signaled for the squad to stop. We watched the wounded and dying. The hootches were either completely leveled or burning. One of the west end grenade traps exploded. Two gooks came running from the river on the south side of the village. Molinari and Castanaro dropped them. After the activity subsided, I had the squad spread out to locate any potential intelligence and destroy any remaining supplies. I crossed the road to check out the small boats tied up there. There were only three. White had seen five maybe six boats earlier. I shot out the boat hulls with my shotgun. The concentrated buckshot at close range made six-inch-wide holes in the boat bottoms rendering them useless for further escape by any survivors hiding in the hills.

"Lt. we got an NVA officer over here!" yelled Larson.

I hustled over to where Larson was standing over a headless body in an NVA uniform. I searched his pockets and found a packet of documents, a wallet, and Marlboro cigarettes, probably taken off an Army or Marine casualty. We knew that most POW's were downed flyboys in North Vietnam. Here, in the south the VC and NVA had no real capability to take prisoners, so they executed them. We felt it only fair to leave no survivors.

The documents were in Vietnamese and I had no idea what they said, but they looked important and I would deliver them to Lt.Col. Fagan. There were now no survivors in the village although I felt that some of the villagers had gone down river in the missing boats and there certainly could be some more hiding in the thick forest. I called in to update Lt.Col. Fagan on the effectiveness of the airstrike and our mop up. Guadanoli's squad had survived an intense firefight up on Route 614 with no squad casualties. They had 17 confirmed kills and were very low on ammo. They were being extracted and would beat us back to base.

It had been a productive two days. Now, I needed to lead the squad to a safe extraction point, call in the coordinates, and get back safely to Freedom Hill.

Always expect the unexpected.

Larson, on point, held up his hand. Crouching behind ferns, I could make out shadowy movement coming down the trail that we were on. We had nowhere to go. Surprise was on our side and we would need to press that advantage. The four gooks walked in single file on the narrow trail. They wore basket packs and the first in line carried an AK-47 with a banana clip. Incredibly, they walked to within 5 meters of us. I took out the first one in line and Larson took the last one. Molinari and Castanaro dropped the other two.

Our good luck was still with us. We hurried downhill to our extraction point. The Slick or transport helicopter arrived at the opening just as we did to take us back to our base at Freedom Hill.

The siege at Khe Sanh was over and the Marines were withdrawing. It just seemed to me that when our forces took enemy territory, we should hold it and deny the enemy its use and resources. The powers that be seemed to continually take ground and then desert the hard won territory allowing the enemy to reclaim it for their use. It went against the military tactics that I had studied that was to win ground and hold it. Strategy decisions were way above my pay grade.

We began to scour the Oklahoma ridges to rid the VC mortar caches and intimidate the mortar crews where they lived. I was out with Alpha Squad looking for a VC camp that had been active on Hill 52 when we stumbled onto an NVA (North Vietnamese Army) base camp. Badly outnumbered, I called in coordinates for an airstrike as we made tracks out of there. The heavily forested, steep terrain made for slow, arduous going.

Our movement had been detected and I knew that we were being pursued. We needed to gain the high ground at the top of the ridge where we had a better defensive position and could, hopefully, call in air support to beat back the NVA and extract us. Molinari was our last man to reach the top. We dug in behind whatever natural protection that we could find. I called in our position and was told that a gunship and a slick were scrambling. We had to hold our position for about 10 minutes until the air support arrived.

We could hear the NVA closing distance to our position as they made their way through the heavy underbrush. We were spread along the ridge top in a small clearing that I judged to be barely large enough for a Huey to extract us. Visibility was at best 10-15 meters beyond the edge of the clearing. I could hear the Bell UH-1 Hueys approaching and made radio contact as the NVA opened fire on us. The Huey gunship fired rockets into the jungle's edge below us and unleashed withering machine gun fire. The slick followed in with the door gunner firing to extract us.

I was thanking whatever gods maybe for the fast air coverage and the pilot's ability and guts to extract us from a really small clearing, when Larson slumped over. He had been hit by small arms fire on the left side of his chest probably puncturing his left lung. Adrenaline and some help from White had got him on board the chopper. White ripped open the first aid kit and did what he could. Fortunately, we would back at Freedom Hill in minutes and the corpsman would be waiting to take care of Larson.

The 7th Marines were ready to initiate a clear and destroy operation in the Oklahoma Hills. With the 51st Regiment of the ARVN (Army of the Republic of Vietnam), they would successfully clear the NVA units out of their base camps and infiltration routes in the hills and valleys of Quang Nam Province, particularly the Happy Valley and Charlie Ridge. Our job here was done. The Marines would continue the large scale operation into May 1969.

CHAPTER 28

Back to the Swamp

July 1968

General Westmoreland returned to Washington as the Army Chief of Staff. General Abrams took over MACV (Military Assistance Command Vietnam). We received orders back to My Tho in the Mekong Delta. It was cool. We had extensive experience in the Rung Sat Special Zone and knew the river system around My Tho.

We were ferried to Saigon on a Chinook CH-47 helicopter doing a medical supply run and then hitched a bus ride with the Army to My Tho. I was back in familiar territory. Operation Jackstay had concluded. The Sac Forest of some 400 square miles of mangrove swamp and interlocking streams had been the target of the joint American and South Vietnamese program to clear the Viet Cong sanctuary of arms factories and camps in the thick vegetation.

A new operation called Sea Lords was now in the final planning stage. It was conceived by Admiral Zumwalt, Commander, Naval Forces, Vietnam. The objective was to interdict VC infiltration routes from Cambodia along the river system from the Bassac River to the

Gulf of Thailand and the pacification and clearance of the Bassac Islands. Because of the success of two previous operations, Game Warden and Market Time, this was the primary remaining supply route through the river and canal system from Cambodia into the Mekong Delta.

The Mobile Riverine Assault Force was patrolling the junction of Vam Co and Soirap rivers in the southeastern district of Long An Province. My platoon inserted in the Le Hong Phong Secret Zone 20 miles northeast of Phan Thiet to reconnoiter. Bravo Squad, led by Chief Guadanoli, was sneaking and peeking to our east and Alpha Squad moved south along their flank. We joined up on schedule at 1800 hours. Bravo squad had found a small enemy installation near the river. I called in the coordinates of the VC installation. The plan was for us to stay clear and the Navy would move into the area and provide bombardment to destroy the encampment. We would then mop up after the attack.

The installation was destroyed by Naval gunfire in the morning. It was devastating even from a safe kilometer away. After the attack, we moved in to capture and detain survivors. There were four Viet Cong coming down the trail toward us as we approached the destroyed and still burning camp. Three of them raised their hands in surrender. The fourth tried to escape and Molinari promptly shot and killed her. She was a leader of the local Viet Cong women's association. Among her possessions, we found a medal with the likeness of North Vietnamese President Ho Chi Minh.

Following the trail to the still burning VC camp, we found no other enemy survivors. HQ wanted the three VC prisoners brought in for interrogation and scheduled a patrol boat to extract us. The VC prisoners rode back with us on the PBR.

Two days later, I was out with Alpha Squad on a similar operation in the eastern Kien Hoa province. White was om point as we moved along a trail that paralleled the bank of Bong Ca Creek, about 45 kilometers or 28 miles southeast of Ben Tre. White motioned for us to take cover. There was heavy brush along the side of the trail opposite the creek. Three Viet Cong were coming down the trail. White was closest to them and at 10 meters he opened up with full automatic fire with his M60. Two were killed and the third ran off, but he left a serious blood trail. Molinari and I followed the blood trail. I was a good tracker and could move quietly in pursuit. Within 150 meters we found him lying face down. He had succumbed from his wounds. I searched him for any useful intel, but found nothing.

We found documents on the dead VC that appeared to show the infrastructure of the Viet Cong cadre in Kien Hoa and Go Cong provinces. We also found some very interesting chart overlays, training, and equipment manuals. It was obvious that there were several installations including training facilities in the area. I called for extraction. We had stumbled onto a target rich area that required additional planning and resources. HQ was very interested in the documents that we had found.

The beginning of July had been productive. We had a lot to follow up on and I had both squads scheduled to insert back in the Bong Ca Creek area. With the information that we had found, I was able to select specific targets for harassment and destruction.

July 11, we inserted shortly before midnight. Guadanoli took his squad northwest about a kilometer and established an ambush site. At 0200 they opened fire on an unlighted sampan, killing the four Viet Cong onboard. Bravo squad then moved a short distance southeast and found another unlighted sampan and killed two VC occupants. The VC were transporting supplies at night to avoid the river patrols.

After Guadanoli's squad had contact with the enemy, he estimated that at least seven Viet Cong had returned fire in their direction from the opposite north bank of the river. Guadanoli then led the squad southeast to rendezvous with me and Alpha Squad. We had gone northwest and moved back to meet Bravo squad. Guadanoli and I set up a hastily laid plan for an ambush on the north side of the river.

First, we had to cross the river undetected. The river was a tributary that was approximately 20 meters across. I waded out and quickly found that it was over 6 feet deep. There wasn't much of current and we swam across.

We found a small trail along the edge of the north bank. We crept quietly down the trail and found their camp. As we laid in wait, some Viet Cong on the south bank opened fire on something and the VC on the north bank returned fire on their comrades. I heard several cries of pain from their friendly fire. We were still undetected and initiated our ambush about 5 minutes later. We killed one VC and wounded several that crawled off into the heavy brush in the dark.

After waiting quietly in the dark for any additional targets of opportunity, we finally withdrew from the area at dawn. Molinari had sprained his left ankle, but we had no casualties. We found a quiet spot on the river and called for extraction at 0615 hours. White and Molinari posted at opposite sides of the extraction point. We had our breakfast and waited for the boat.

CHAPTER 29

Ben Tre

August 1968

Ben Tre is the capitol city of Kien Hoa Province and is located on Bao Island about 85 kilometers southeast of Saigon and about 20 minutes down river from My Tho. The Viet Cong had taken over the city during the Tet Offensive and it had been bombed heavily. The 9th Infantry Battalion had retaken the city, but it had been intense house-to-house fighting against a well-dug in enemy.

The surviving Viet Cong had retreated to the small surrounding villages that were sympathetic to the VC. The village chieftains that were not sympathetic were publicly executed by the VC.

We got the job of searching out and destroying the sympathetic villages. Psychologically, we were to terrorize them and thereby, hopefully, keep them from taking over the rest of the villages. Our first target was a small village northwest of Ben Tre city along Route 60 towards Chau Thanh. It was a 5 kilometer walk from Ben Tre. We left the newly established Army Base at 2100 hours after a nice hot dinner thanks to the 9th Infantry battalion stationed there.

The temperature had dropped into the 70's and the rain had stopped. I fully expected to run into some local traffic as we walked single file keeping 5 meters apart. The night was dark and quiet. White had the lead and I was last in line.

Twenty minutes into our trek, White halted our advance. He had seen the flicker of a light far ahead around a bend in the road. The 9th Infantry had a mine sweeping team that swept Route 60 every morning and it was regularly mined and booby trapped at night by the VC. White reported that the VC were less than 150 meters ahead and about 60 meters around the bend in the road ahead. It was too dark to navigate the heavy brush and forest. I decided that we should avoid the road surface. It could already be mined. Creeping along both sides of the road around the bend, we got a view of the VC mine crew ahead operating with the light from two lanterns. We opened with full automatic fire and heard cries of pain. A figure came into view by the lantern on the left and that VC was quickly shot.

We carefully advanced keeping to the edge of the brush. When I got closer, I could make out three dead Viet Cong in the lantern light. They had four hand-made "dap loi" or step on mines made from empty .50 caliber shells filled with metal shrapnel, sealed in wax, and placed in a bamboo cylinder with a nail in the bottom to serve as a firing pin when stepped on. After searching the bodies and finding nothing of intelligence value, we disabled the mines. We found no footprints or other evidence of any other VC's that may have escaped our attack. It was reasonable to assume that this was just a three-man mine crew.

I was concerned that the attack was heard in the VC village up ahead and that more mines may have been planted in the road between here and the village. I moved into the brush on the south side of the road. We would sneak and peek our way to the village perimeter. I half expected that a squad of VC would come down the road to investigate the gunfire.

We paralleled the road all the way to the village and encountered no other VC. It was 0215 and the trees were dripping from a passing rain shower. The VC villager was quiet and we could discern no sentries. I sent White, Larson, and Molinari around to the east. Castanaro and Connell stayed with me. It was a simple plan. We would lob grenades into the hootches and then open fire on the VC's as they exited. We would empty our clips and then disappear back on the bush and return to the base.

Our attack was very loud and short. Our plan was to kill a few and terrorized the rest. I reported back in before breakfast and filed my after action report. The 9th Infantry would send a mine sweeping team along with a full platoon this morning to clear the road and then visit the village. Maybe the Army could win their hearts and minds. My job was to kill the enemy and terrorize the sympathizers to prevent additional VC support and to thwart additional recruits from going over to the Viet Cong.

I was filled in on our next target VC village and we had until tomorrow to rest up and plan for our next nighttime foray.

I slept for four hours and then reviewed the maps and intelligence that had been gathered on our target village. A road that we called Route 885 ran southeast from Ben Tre City to Giong Trom and the village was on a bend in the road that was close to a creek. Since the entire province averages only 3 meters above sea level, there were many little creeks and tidal flow often submerged large land areas. Our target village was called Cao Boi or as we said "Cowboy". It was on a tributary that ran through Ben Tre to the Ham Luong River. I checked with the Mobile Riverine Force and they felt positive that a small SEAL Team Assault Boat (STAB) could navigate the creek.

This would provide a more stealthy approach than motoring some 12 kilometers down Route 885. I met with Chief Guadanoli, Bravo Squad Leader. He agreed that a river insertion made more sense and that we could insert closer to our target. We wanted to insert in the wee hours. Hit our target hard and disappear in the night.

Chief Guadanoli said, "LT, we can hit the village within 20 minutes of insertion and be back for extraction within 45 minutes. In and out fast."

I really had a difficult time ordering Bravo Squad to go without me. As Officer-in-Charge of the Platoon that consisted of two squads, they were my responsibility. Deep inside I felt that I should be there. Chief Guadanoli was as good as they come and had more in-country experience than I had, but still it was my responsibility. The STAB was a 21-foot Boston Whaler that could transport a six-man squad plus two crewmen. There wasn't room for one more and I had other responsibilities with Alpha Squad.

While Bravo Squad was going downriver, I would take Alpha Squad northwest toward the city of Binh Cong. There was a VC camp on the southeastern side of the city and it was indicated in some captured intelligence that there was a supply of ordnance there that included rockets and ammunition. We would insert from the Ham Luong River.

White, Castanaro, Larson, Molinari, Connell, and I were inserted by a STAB piloted by a young petty officer named Young. After our insertion, Young would return to My Tho and stand by for our extraction call. We slowly and quietly drifted past Binh Cong and the anchored sampans. We landed just 400 meters south along a small tributary stream. The tide was in and the brown water covered the forest floor as we worked our way toward the VC camp that should be only a short distance upriver. I hate snakes and I thoroughly believed that every venomous snake in the world lived in the Mekong Delta. My mind was wandering thinking about snakes as we waded our way towards the camp. I had to force myself to focus on the mission. Inattention could be fatal.

Finally, at 0330 hours we came to dry ground. My dead reckoning put us very close the VC camp and supply cache. White had been our point man and he came back for relief.

"LT, there is no sign of a camp up ahead. I can usually smell them or the smoke from their fires, but nothing yet."

It had been a hard slog to get here and it was time for us to check for leeches anyway. It was a good place to take a short rest. I passed the word to take 10. It was, of course, raining. Heavy rain was to be expected and then some sunshine during the day with extreme humidity. It wasn't worth the effort of putting on a poncho because we would get soaked anyway and the poncho could make some noise in the brush that could give away our position. That could be deadly. Better to be wet.

The encampment was supposed to be on this tributary creek that we had been following. In the pre-dawn darkness, the parakeets and monkeys began their wake up calls. A pair of large sarus cranes were raucously greeting the day. It reminded me of my early morning deer hunts with my dad in Wyoming years ago as the forest came to life at dawn.

My mind was wandering again and that's dangerous. Focus. Do your job and keep your guys alive. Our point man, Castanaro, held up his hand. I could smell it too. We were very close. The VC in the camp would be starting their morning ablutions and stirring about.

"Mau len"!

We all heard it loud and clear. A commanding voice in Vietnamese saying hurry up. A two-way heated discussion in rapid Vietnamese followed that I could not translate. I guessed that the loud male voice was berating his wife or girlfriend over something. A female in the typical black pajamas emerged from the nearest hootch to light a breakfast fire. The male then came out and walked to the edge of the creek and pissed.

Then, I got a really bad feeling when a dog trotted out in our direction and began barking.

Armed VC came out of the hootches. We opened fire. White's M60 strafed the area. I shot the guy pissing in the river. I saw two other VC hit. There were nine other VC firing into the forest. Larson and Molinari lobbed grenades. I signaled the squad to vamoose as the grenades exploded giving us some cover.

I called for Young to meet us at the predetermined extraction point at 0600 hours. It would take us that long to get back there. The tide was going out and we stayed close to the creek in knee deep water. I guessed that the VC might come searching in their sampans along the creek. They could move much faster than we could wade. Our luck held. We created enough surprise and disruption that nobody came looking. Young was waiting for us when we arrived.

After boarding the STAB, we all did a search for leeches. When Larson dropped his fatigues, I saw a fair amount of blood on his left thigh running down his leg.

"LT, I got scratched back there. An AK round ricocheted off a tree and took out a small chunk of meat".

Molinari wrapped the superficial wound and Larson would have the corpsman at My Tho disinfect it.

After a shower and a change of clothes, I filed my after action report and anxiously waited for Bravo Squad to check in. It was a long wait until communications came requesting extraction with two wounded.

Two corpsman (USN Medics) met the boat as it docked back at My Tho. Chief Guadanoli had been hit under his left arm and was in very serious condition. Rivera had stepped on a mine and his right foot was a bloody mess. Somehow the other four squad members had got them back and kept them alive.

They're my brothers. Maybe if I had been with Bravo squad I could have made a difference. Rivera's right foot was mangled and would be amputated. Guadanoli had a sucking chest wound and was fighting for his life.

Man, I've got to change jobs.

C H A P T E R 3 0

Riding the Boats

September 1968

My platoon was shorthanded. Guadanoli had been flown stateside after a week in the hospital in Saigon to stabilize the wound to his left lung. Rivera's right foot was amputated at the ankle. He had significant healing and rehab ahead. Larson's scratch had been treated by the corpsman on the base and he was fine.

I had split the platoon into two squads of four men each to ride with the boat crews to interdict piracy and the VC logistical support routes. The boat crews were very happy to have us with them. We were the boarding party to search the sampans and junks that were intercepted.

I really loved riding the boats, probably, because I grew up so far away from the water. I soon found out just how deceptive and dangerous the job was when we boarded a suspicious sampan on the Ham Luong River.

September and October are the transition months into the dry season in the Mekong Delta and are characterized by violent thunder storms with heavy rain. We boarded PBF-16, a Swift boat captained by LTJG Johns in a downpour. Under the cover of darkness, we would proceed downriver to a point near Lao Dat Island. There had been reports of junks coming upriver with VC supplies and ordnance. The boat captain said that we would stay in the dark shadow of the island ready to intercept any passing boat traffic.

The ride downriver had been uneventful. The rain had stopped before the first rays of dawn. We were quietly idling just off the west side of Lao Dat only about 10 meters from shore. A junk came around the southern tip of the island motoring upriver. The captain immediately ordered general quarters and hit the throttles.

The junk turned downriver, but had no chance of outrunning the 50-foot Swift boat powered by twin diesels. LTJG Johns quickly maneuvered and intercepted the junk. Gunners Mate Ward on the forward twin .50 caliber machine guns fired a warning shot across the junk's bow. Larson jumped on board the junk as we came along side. I covered the two gooks on deck with my 12-gauge shotgun. Keane and Molinari jumped onto the junk amidships.

The VC at the helm of the junk tossed a grenade into the cockpit of the Swift boat behind LTJG John and the other gook grabbed a rifle from the bow. I shot the VC as the grenade left his hand just a split second too late. Larson killed the other one before he could raise the AK-47 and fire a shot.

LTJG Johns and I dove into the brown river. Keane, Molinari, and Larson hit the deck of the junk as grenade went off. Gunners Mate Ward was protected by armor plating around the forward gun turret. The Quartermaster on the aft machine gun caught most of the blast.

The boat captain and I climbed back on board. The Quartermaster had no chance. There were some other scratches and bruises, but nothing serious. My trusty Ithaca shotgun was at the bottom of the river.

We found mortars, grenades, and ammunition stashed on board the junk. The PCF had extensive cockpit damage. Most of the electronics, including the radar, were destroyed. The port side of the forward cockpit was severely damaged along with everything that had been there. The engines were still running and the engineman reported that all power was functional. The captain and Ward worked on the helm as we hooked up the junk to be towed in.

I'm a believer in miracles after Ward and LTJG Johns were able to restore steerage out the wreckage. We had a slow and somber trip back upriver towing the junk. PBF-16 and the surviving crew members were heading to the Bassac River base for repairs.

Our river duty would continue. Most of the river traffic was normal. We would intercept, search, check papers and wish the locals well on their trip to market or good luck fishing.

CHAPTER 31

Operation Sea Lords

October 1968

Sea Lords launched October 8, 1968. The operation was intended to disrupt North Vietnamese supply lines around the Mekong Delta. The waterways were the logistical supply routes used to infiltrate men and ordnance from Cambodia. Conceived by Vice Admiral Zumwalt, Commander, Naval Forces, Vietnam (COMNAVFORV) as a joint operation with the South Vietnamese.

My job was to concentrate on two islands on the Bassac River, Tan Dinh and Dung. Both islands were VC strongholds. The Bassac River flows from Phnom Penh, Cambodia into Vietnam and feeds the Mekong. Dung Island was our first target. The Marines had just hit Dung hard with airstrikes on the suspected VC camps and the Navy Swift boats had been hitting the villages near the shore with daily 81mm rocket attacks and machine gun fire.

I held a platoon meeting and reviewed the maps and photos that we had available of Dung Island. Our objective was to find and destroy any ordnance caches on the island. The Marines, 9th Army

Division, and ARVN forces were canvassing both shore lines of the Bassac River while we cleared the islands. There was a shore side village near a rocky beach that had been pretty much leveled by earlier strikes. It looked secluded from other encampments and should be a good insertion point. From there, we could then reconnoiter south and cover the long and narrow land mass. Some Sea Wolves support would be available to us from a Mobile Riverine ship about 7 minutes of airtime away.

The Sea Wolves were the Navy Helicopter Attack Squadron based on ships (LST's) that served as bases for the Mobile Riverine Force in the rivers. The LST's had helicopter launching pads and enabled the Navy to provide air support close to operations in the Mekong Delta. The helicopter gunships could be scrambled to support special warfare operations in the Rung Sat Special Zone from LST's that had been strategically positioned in a nearby navigable river.

We boarded a PBR from River Assault Division (RAD) 92 for our insertion on Dung Island at 1700 hours. The boat caption, Chief Walden, had been skirting ambushes on the river for the past week and let us know that he would be in the dead center of the river at full throttle until we reached Dung Island. We climbed aboard and hung on as Chief Walden got us underway for a fast ride upriver. It was a short ride to Dung Island and the boat captain nosed us in by the rocky beach just south of the bombed out village.

White jumped in first. The brown water was knee deep. I was next followed by Molinari, Larson, Keane, and Connell. We scrambled across the beach to the tree line of coconut palms. I always felt more secure in the forest. Separating about five meters apart, I led the squad toward the destroyed village on the river bank.

It was very quiet in the growing twilight. We slowly approached the village watching and listening, but nothing – no VC and no critters of any kind. It was eerily quiet. Too quiet. I got that oh shit feeling and motioned the squad to take defensive positions. We waited and watched, but not for long.

I clearly heard the bolt of a rifle snap shut. The VC had heard or observed our insertion. The ambush was set to catch us by surprise as we entered the bombed out village. We had come in very quietly through the bush and I believed that they did not know that we were here yet. The snick of the rifle bolt was most likely a VC jacking a shell into the chamber. He probably carried the AK-47 with an empty chamber and needed to jack in a round from the 30-round clip to be loaded and ready to fire.

I decided that we would quietly wait. We were trained to have the patience of predators. I was guessing that the VC were less patient and we could turn this into our ambush. The minutes passed and it was getting darker. My squad was disciplined and battle hardened. We waited barely breathing. In the growing darkness I could just make out a VC slowly walking into the clearing from the north side. He carefully inspected the trail leading into the village where the VC had been expecting us to arrive. We had sneaked and peeked through the bush and left no footprints or sign of passing on the trail. Satisfied that we had not passed by, the VC scout waved to his comrades. Three other VC came into the clearing and conferred with the scout rapidly speaking and pointing up the trail.

The VC scout was closest to me and I shot him. The squad opened fire and there were four dead or dying VC at the trail head. The Green Faces will live to fight another day. Our good luck was still with us. We checked the bodies for any useful intel and looked over the destroyed village. We collected the rifles and ammo from the dead VC and threw them into the river.

White took the point and we headed back into the bush. We worked our way due east about a kilometer in the dark. Reaching a slightly elevated grove of palms, I signaled a stop. It was a good place for us to rest until daybreak. I wanted to find our way over to the eastern shore of the island in the morning to reconnoiter a suspected camp that appeared on aerial photos.

About 0400 hours a violent thunder storm rolled in. I was seated under a palm tree leaning against the trunk with my boonie hat pulled down as low as possible. It was impossible to stay dry or comfortable. The Mekong Delta is crawling with snakes of every kind, including many poisonous varieties. Molinari awoke next to me with a muffled expletive. A 5-foot python slithered over his legs. Grabbing the big reptile behind the head, Molinari pulled his knife and sliced through the serpent severing its head. He whispered to me that he had breakfast for the squad. Tastes like chicken.

The rain stopped just after dawn, but the clouds were heavy and dark. The morning fog limited visibility, but also provided us cover to search the eastern river bank. Two hours later we had searched southward along the river and found nothing. It was over 90 degrees Fahrenheit and very humid. After a short break, Larson volunteered to take the point and we continued along the eastern shore of the island.

By mid-afternoon the storm clouds were gathering for our daily drenching when I smelled a camp nearby. Checking the aerial photos, this camp was near the southern-most tip of Dung Island and there should be several sampans tied to a small wharf. It could be a small fishing village or it could a VC camp on the Cambodian supply line. I had a whispered discussion with the squad and set up positions on the north and western camp perimeter. We would observe the camp activities before approaching and entering the clearing.

We watched and waited as the minutes ticked by. It became a couple of hours. The afternoon rain started. Still there was very little activity in the camp. We were soaked, uncomfortable, and getting itchy for some action. The patience of a predator finally paid off. Three pajama-clad figures came up the muddy dirt road leading to the camp. They were all carrying weapons. I didn't know the population of the camp, but had to assume that we were significantly outnumbered. I made the decision to call in the coordinates for an airstrike and lead the squad safely away.

The Sea Wolves got the message. The helicopter gunships hit the camp after we got about kilometer away. The rocket explosions were music to our ears. We reached the southernmost tip of Dung Island. This was our extraction point and we took defensive positions to await our ride. It was getting dark. The PBR (Patrol Boat, River) that was scheduled to extract us was overdue.

Just as I was calling command, the PBR came into view in the twilight. After we boarded, the boat captain, Chief Walters, told me that they had received fire and had spent some time neutralizing the incoming. The rain stopped and we had an uneventful ride back to base.

In the morning, I had a meeting with the joint command for Operation Sea Lords. It was evident that after clearing the major threat on Dung Island that the strategy required the elimination of the remaining VC threat on Tan Dinh Island to the north. The Mobile Riverine Group Bravo would be mounting lightning raids on the enemy-held coastal waterways. Task Force 115 PCF's (Swift Boats) would be attacking the island's shoreline camps. Our job was to mop up and destroy remaining enemy ordnance and any surviving Viet Cong. Allied naval and ground forces could then proceed unmolested upriver.

I briefed the remaining members of my under-sized platoon that afternoon on our mission to Tan Dinh Island. We were nearing the end of our tour of duty and I was expecting a replacement platoon to relieve us at any time. I reminded everyone that we needed to stay focused one day at a time. Task Force 115 was hitting the island tomorrow with air support from the Sea Wolves. We would insert the day after as the 3rd Brigade, 9th Infantry Division would move onto the dry land east of the island.

The assault on Tan Dinh was planned to occur in several waves of heavy shore bombardment and airstrikes. I reviewed the reports of the attack and aerial photos that evening. There were three VC supply depots identified. If we encountered Viet Cong in large numbers, it was too much to cover in one day even with air support readily available. I suggested and received authorization to change our plan into two separate missions. We would insert on the western side of the island and reconnoiter the two camps located there. The Vietnamese Marines would have a platoon inserted to reconnoiter the VC camp on the other side of Tan Dinh Island.

We inserted in the dense morning fog. By 0930 hours, we had gone over the first camp on the western shore. It was decimated and smelled of explosives and dead flesh. We found 15 bodies that were bloated and black. The maggots and critters were having a feed. We rounded up the weapons and a few rounds of ammunition that we destroyed. There was a dirt track leading north toward the second camp on this side of the island and it had some blood trails from yesterday's survivors.

I took the point and slowly worked our way toward the next camp. It was less than a kilometer. I followed the edge of trail carefully sneaking and peeking. The rest of the platoon followed in single file with White bringing up the rear. Approaching the still smoking remnants of the VC camp, I could see several VC sitting under the remains of a hootch with a sagging thatch roof and only some bamboo poles holding it up. The eight remaining men in my platoon knew exactly what to do with a couple of hand signals. Larson was next to me. He had played baseball in high school and had been a stand out pitcher in American Legion ball. We both launched M61 grenades into the hootch.

The M61 fragmentation grenade was lethal to 5 meters and casualty producing to 15 meters or about 49 feet. I could throw one about 45 meters.

The platoon opened fire at targets of opportunity when the grenades exploded. It was over in less than a minute. We held our defensive positions. We watched and waited for any movement or VC support to show. It was quiet and the VC were no longer writhing in their death throes. Carefully, we began searching the camp. The airstrike had been effective. There was a major cache of ordnance, rice, and medical supplies that had been hit. We blew up the cache and made certain that the remnants had no functionality.

The camp had a good river landing and I called in our position for extraction. White and Larson took positions on the north and south as we waited for our pick up. Our extraction vessel arrived. I had not seen any river craft like it. The boat captain, Chief Robertson, explained to me on the ride back that this was an LSSC (Light SEAL Support Craft). The LSSC was a new addition to the Riverine Mobile Force. It was about 24 feet long with a 9.5-foot beam. It was powered by twin Ford 427 gas engines powering Jacuzzi water jets for shallow water capability. It had two single-mounted 7.62 mm machine guns and a .50 caliber Browning machine gun. Due to heavier construction, it was not as exposed to penetrating damage from small arms fire.

C H A P T E R 3 2

Back to the States

November 1968

Operation SeaLords was beginning to hamper the Communist resupply to the Plain of Reeds as the Mekong Delta was known to them. In the first phase of SeaLords, allied forces established patrol barriers using electronic sensors along the river system that paralleled the Cambodian border. In early November, the Swift boats and river assault craft had opened up the Bassac River at Long Xuyen and the canals at Rach Gia. Our work in destroying the island camps and weapons caches had greatly reduced the VC interdiction of river traffic. The next step was to cut infiltration routes from the Parrot's Beak area of Cambodia that supported heavy Communist operations west of Saigon.

We were assigned to assist a Vietnamese paramilitary unit in the area of the Vam Co Tay River. We would patrol the waterways and canals aboard the river assault craft. There was a heavy enemy concentration there and our job was to interdict supplies to the enemy ground forces. My shorthanded platoon looked at this as favorable duty. No slogging through the mangrove swamps or sneaking and peeking through the rain forest.

After a week of riding on Swift boats and boarding sampans, our orders came through to return to the states. The replacement platoon reported in and we caught a lift to Tan Son Huit airport in Saigon. The corpsman had supplied me with a large amount of anti-fungal cream for the pervasive jungle rot on my feet and privates. The prolonged immersion in less than pure water created a perfect bacterial environment for it. It itched and was ugly. Before the long flight to Hawaii, I coated everything with the cream. At Hickham Field in Hawaii, my platoon boarded a Military Air Transport to Travis Air Base in Fairfield, California in between San Francisco and Sacramento. From there, we had several options to go south to the base in Coronado. Some of the guys elected to use accumulated leave time to go home. Molinari and I signed up for a flight to Halsey Field at the Naval Air Station on North Island in San Diego. We would have a day to kill before the scheduled flight to Coronado.

I had a day to kill in Northern California and convinced Molinari to tour the state capitol in Sacramento with me. I figured that it would be less stressful than anywhere closer to Berkeley. I had heard that the state capitol building was spectacular. I was also concerned that Molinari would head into the San Francisco area and the hot bed of anti-war sentiment.

I rented a car. I splurged and rented a Mustang convertible for our trip to Sacramento. It was a beautiful, bright sunny day in Northern California and I drove through the dry land farming area to Route 80 through Vacaville. I found the capitol building and, as luck would have it, we arrived just in time for a guided tour. Even Molinari was impressed with the murals of the gold rush. After the tour, we headed back to the car to find a restaurant. There was a group of college age "flower children" assembled in front of the state capitol. Molinari and I were both in uniform and became immediate targets. The scruffy young men and pretty girls yelled ugly epithets at us. We were two days out of the swamp. Welcome home, assholes.

Molinari snapped when one of the bearded, disheveled young men grabbed his arm while screaming baby killer. In less than a heartbeat, Molinari dispatched him. He was bleeding and rolling on the ground in pain. The capitol police came running with guns drawn to break it up.

A couple of hours later, I was driving back to Travis Air Base, but Molinari was being held with charges pending. A much decorated war hero who had survived to return home after being in harm's way to protect freedom had been arrested. I called Commander Kaufman in Coronado to see what could be done to help one of our own. After hearing me out, the Commander told me to get back to base.

Three days from the Rung Sat Special Zone, I arrived in Coronado, California. I checked in and found out that Molinari had been released and was enroute to Coronado. Cmdr. Kaufman had pulled some strings. After reporting in and getting settled in BOQ (Bachelor Officers Quarters), I retrieved my Ford Galaxy 500 convertible from storage. I drove north to the Big O Tires store on Garnet Avenue near Pacific Beach. After an oil change, lube, and overall check, it was time for me to buy some civilian clothes. Next stop was Macy's on Horton Avenue. I never was much of a shopper and in 20 minutes had found a pair of chino slacks, Levi's jeans, and four Polo shirts. The cashier was a very pretty blonde with flashing blue eyes and freckles. She flashed me a radiant smile as I fumbled with my wallet to pay my bill. I was in uniform so she knew I was a naval officer.

She said, "Are you based here in San Diego"?

"Yes, ma'am." I handed her three twenty dollar bills got my $3.48 change and started to leave.

She said, "My name is Eddi. Come back again".

I was tongue tied as usual around pretty girls, but I knew that I wanted to know more about her. There were no other customers around, so I hesitated at her station. I was looking at her, but my mouth wasn't working.

She said, "You're looking at my name tag that says Edna. That's my given name and the Department of Human Services at Macy's only puts our given names on our name tags, but all my friends and family call me Eddi, besides I used to work at Eddie's Diner".

All I could muster was, "Have a good day".

I mentally kicked myself all the way back to base for not having the gumption to ask her out or least get her phone number. I parked at the administration building and got an updated base sticker for my car. Then it was time for a cold beer at the Officers Club. I recognized a big Marine at the O Club bar.

"Hey, Major Cashin."

"Hey, yourself, Indian, only from now on it's Dick. Tomorrow is my last day on active duty and I'm shipping out in the morning. I have a new job in Thailand. You might have some interest".

The Major explained over two cold Corona's that he was resigning his commission and leaving the Marine Corps for a new job with the Company, as he referred to the CIA. He would be based initially in Bangkok. He went into some detail about how much money he would making without being shot at on most days. He made a good pitch for me to follow him and said he would provide a good referral to his boss. There was a certain attraction to staying out the vile mangrove swamp where I had been making my living. We commiserated about the misleading news on the war and the hatred on the college campuses and general population for military personnel. I still felt like I owed the Navy and my best friends, tried and true, were in the teams. In combat, you really find out the measure and character of men and who is reliable. I probably counted about 20 men that I knew I could really depend on. How many civilians could match that?

I wished the Major all the best and went back to BOQ (Bachelor Officers Quarters). After my second hot shower of the day, I was looking forward to about 12 hours of uninterrupted sleep. The beautiful and upbeat cashier at Macy's, Eddi, was vividly on my mind. I would need to take some action and, probably, be emotionally prepared for a letdown. Most pretty young women had been convinced by their college professors, their long-haired liberal boyfriends, and the media that we were baby killers and should be loathed. I would have to learn how to deal with the undisciplined civilians. Maybe someday, but for now I definitely preferred the dedicated and disciplined military personnel serving for God, honor, and country.

I woke up feeling more refreshed and well-rested than I had in months. There were no mortar rounds in the middle of the night in San Diego. After a morning run and a short work out in the gym, I decided that I really needed another pair of Levi's and a trip to Macy's was on my plan of the day. I showered and dressed in my new civilian clothes and headed downtown. Eddi was there at the cash register in the Men's Department as I approached.

She flashed me a smile and I noticed again how her bright, blue eyes sparkled, as she said, "Hey there, you're back".

As I fumbled for a response, she said, "Are you going to ask me out?"

We agreed that tonight at 6:00 PM I would pick her up for dinner. Eddi wrote her address and phone number on my sales receipt. I was elated and hopelessly infatuated.

I reported to Cmdr. Kauffman at 14:30. My orders, as expected, would keep me stateside. I would be in charge of administration for the training unit. Basically, this entailed administrative responsibility for SEALs in training for Team One on the west coast. It would, also, give me the opportunity to pursue the lovely Miss Eddi.

Two month's into my new role, I was settled into my new routine. Chief Foster was the yeoman assigned to my unit and like most Chief Petty Officers in the Navy, he was an experienced and steady hand. There was a shred of truth to the old saying that the chiefs ran the Navy. Miss Eddi was becoming a steady companion and I was beginning to think that this might become a long term relationship.

September 3, 1969, I got the word. Connell, John L, Petty Officer 2nd Class, was killed in action. Connell had been with me since BUD/s in 1965. He had volunteered to go back in country with a new platoon being deployed in July. He had been hit while working with the South Vietnamese Riverine Force interdicting traffic on the Mekong River south of Saigon.

Feeling pretty low, I called Miss Eddi to see if she could have dinner with me. She agreed and we went to the Addison north of San Diego in the Carmel Valley. Her bright smile and sunny disposition always brightened my outlook. Somehow over dinner, she let me know that our relationship was getting more serious. She asked me when I was getting out of the Navy. I tried to explain how I felt that I owed the Navy and that I was not about to become an undisciplined civilian. Things went downhill from there.

She got very serious and said, "Jack, I would love to show you off in uniform. You know that there are places where that wouldn't be wise. My friends from college don't know that you're in the military and I won't tell them. I'm tired of feeling like we 're sneaking around here."

I tried to explain that we were very well-trained and I served with a group of exceptional men. Men that I knew that I could count on in the most difficult situations. Men that were proud to serve their country even if we were derided by the press and on the left wing college campuses.

She countered, "After serving three times in Vietnam, haven't you done enough?"

Over the next few months, Eddi and I continued to see each other, but the issue of my military service was a source of some continuing contention. San Diego was a military town, but I made sure that I was out of uniform whenever we ventured elsewhere. My birthday in December, 1969, came as my current administrative assignment was coming to an end. Over dinner with Miss Eddi, I let her know that I was expecting to receive orders to go back in-country with my brothers.

She looked down and said, "Jack, I know that you're a good officer and dedicated to your men, but you're important to me. Now you're going to leave and I don't know if you'll be back."

I explained that our typical in-country tour of duty was only six months instead of twelve months like the other branches of the military served. Many SEALs were on their fifth tours and if the war continued they could expected to continue to return to combat. She was not pleased to hear this. I was hoping that our relationship would become lifelong, but my service in the Navy was an obvious point of contention.

Man, I may have to change jobs to hold onto the love of life.

I really had to do some deep thinking. After dropping off Miss Eddi, I drove to Mission Beach. I always liked to hear the surf rolling in and crashing on the sand. I needed to take stock. My investment portfolio was still growing from my graduate school days. I wasn't poor, but I had nowhere near enough to retire on. Besides, I was only 28 years old. The more I considered my alternatives the more that felt the resolve to serve my country and not let down my brothers on the team.

CHAPTER 33

Orders

January 1970

My administrative post came to end. Cmdr. Kaufman gave me my orders to assume the responsibility as Officer-in-Charge of Golf Platoon that was now in advanced training. I was physically up to speed and mentally ready. We would ship out at the end of February. It was going to be a little different in-country. President Nixon had initiated a Plan of Vietnamization designed to return the responsibility of defense back to the South Vietnamese. Conventional forces were being withdrawn as control and resources were being transferred to the South Vietnamese ARVN Forces.

The SEALs and many Special Forces units were continuing their support, however. There was a new base created at the tip of the Ca Mau Peninsula. A floating firebase designated Seafloat. It was created by welding 14 barges together. It was accessible by sea and provided a landing area for helicopters. Seafloat would be our new home after arriving in country.

We arrived on March 3, 1970 at the now much upgraded Tan Son Nhut Air Base in Saigon. We passed members of the 3rd Battalion 187th Infantry, 101st Airborne Division assembling for their return to the states. Golf Platoon had bonded in our 7 weeks together. We had almost 500 kilometers to travel to our new base where the Ca Mau Peninsula met the Gulf of Thailand. We would overnight here and then be shuttled to Seafloat by a Chinook tomorrow morning.

A change of orders caught up to me in the early morning. My platoon was being re-directed. The NLF or Communist National Liberation Front had an entrenched position near the Cai Ngay Canal. We were now directed to support the eradication of VC supply depots and to assist the Riverine Units in interdicting the supply line supporting the NLF. We were going back, again, to the area that I knew around My Tho. Back to the river system that I knew very well. It felt like I was going home. We would be working with River Assault Squadron 9. Our operating base would be in Dong Tam, the upgraded My Tho facility. It had been built about 5 kilometers from My Tho because it was the nearest unpopulated area. It was familiar territory, but in the two plus years since I had been in My Tho, there had been major changes. It was now a full logistical support base that could overhaul riverine watercraft and supply smaller installations in the area. There was a huge fuel storage facility and extensive ordnance bunkers.

We got settled in quickly. Two days in-country and Bravo Squad would ride along on PBR-38 to assist in interdicting VC supplies on the tributaries and canals. I would take Alpha Squad upriver to a hamlet halfway to Lap Vo that we called the Halfway House. It was reported to be a VC camp and supply depot. Our Boat Captain, Chief Grattoni, was skimming along in mid-stream. I was standing at the back of the forward twin machine guns holding on to the starboard side of the pilot house when the lights went out.

The Viet Cong on the shore got lucky. We got hit by a rocket. The impact knocked me clear to the bow. Chief Grattoni looked in great pain and the crewman aft was splattered across the deck. Three of my squad were in the brown water. As my head cleared, it was obvious that we were in deep trouble. The engineman yelled to Grattoni that the port engine was gone and the starboard engine was damaged, but he could keep headway with the starboard diesel turning low RPMs. The boat captain was holding onto the wheel to keep himself upright.

Grattoni yelled, "Get your men onboard and let's get out of here."

My legs weren't quite right, but I limped over to the port gunwale that was blown away to just above the waterline and found a line to throw out. Walters grabbed the line with his left hand and latched onto Tessecini's collar with his right. He struggled onboard with my help and then we hoisted Tessecini onto the deck. He had extensive injuries to his left side and arm. Molinari, who had been with me since BUD/s, was floating face down and drifting away with the current.

No hesistation. Ignore the pain in my legs. Just get Molinari. I grabbed the line and jumped into the brown water. Holding the line in my teeth, I did a breast stroke to Molinari and flipped him over. His face was gone and he wasn't breathing. No pulse in his neck. Looped the line around his chest and Walters pulled us in. The current had drifted us out of range and Grattoni got us out to midstream to limp back to Dong Tam.

We finally made it back to base and there was a corpsman was there to meet us. The impact had herniated two discs in Grattoni's lower back and some shrapnel had flayed his left shoulder leaving an open, bleeding gash. Tessecini was being airlifted to Saigon. The aft gunner, a crewman named Brown, was also airlifted out. There was nothing that could be done for the Quartermaster or Molinari. The corpsman cut off my fatigues to treat my legs. He meticulously picked out shards of the fiberglass hull and bits of foreign material from both of my legs for the next 20 minutes. My left knee had been hyper-extended from the impact and I had suffered a concussion. Luckily, every extremity was mostly intact and still working. I would hurt for several days, but I felt that I was still operational.

Man, I've got to change jobs.

My leg wounds had healed after a week, but I still couldn't bear much weight on my left leg. The damaged knee was still painful. It was the same knee that I had hurt back in college playing football in my senior year.

The corpsman advised me to get to the hospital in Saigon where they could professionally evaluate the damage. It was good advice. The Army doctor that reviewed the x-rays told me that I needed orthopedic surgery on my knee or walking would be a long term problem. Never mind running or jumping out of aircraft.

It was a ticket back to the states and most probably would force a change in jobs. I would need to make a sincere effort to deal with the undisciplined civilians. Their rampant dislike and derision of Vietnam War veterans was fueled by the media, celebrities, and the left wing college professors.

Author's Note

There was a significant amount of research that went into this novel in an effort to make it historically accurate. For insight into the Rung Sat Special Zone where many of our Special Forces personnel performed under terrible conditions, I was able to review some of the declassified After Action Reports from the Department of the Navy that were very insightful. Neil Sheehan's, *A Bright Shining Lie: John Paul Vann and America in Vietnam*, were important sources. For information on sniper activity, *Silent Warrior*, by Charles Henderson provided information on Sergeant Carlos Hathcock and sniper methods.

History of the conflict was described for me by Joseph Buttinger in his excellent work titled, *Vietnam: A Dragon Embattled*, Volume I, *From Colonialism to the Vietminh*, Volume II, *Vietnam at War*, New York, Praeger, 1967. Also, George C. Herring's, *America's Longest War, The United States and Vietnam, 1950-1975*, New York: Alfred A. Knopf, 1986.

The river operations were described very well by Major General William B. Fulton in his detailed report, *Riverine Operations 1966-1969*, Washington D.C.; Department of the Army, 1973. Also, the book by Eric Micheletti, *SEALs in Vietnam: U.S. Navy Commandos in the Vietnam War*, January, 2001. *Jane's Fighting Ships*, provided specific details on the river boats and their firepower.

Much of the substantive material came from personal acquaintances and their stories as they remembered them.